The Hou

Evelyn Hunter-Smith, a country rector's daughter, was inclined to be a poor man's edition of Berti Jago. They were extraordinarily alike in many ways. Both were divorcees: Berti had been divorced and Evelyn had divorced her husband, who still paid her a small annuity. They were similar in build except that Evelyn was not quite as tall as Berti and she had a bust, which she considered her best feature. Both were addicted to tight trousers and drink and both had cropped heads — only Evelyn's, which had once been dark, was thick and curly. They had small well-bred faces and rather good noses; but Evelyn's mouth was weak and her teeth inclined to protrude. She was a few years younger than Berti, a fact she mentioned from time to time. Her annuity from her husband was small, only three hundred a year, but she said she had expectations from an elderly aunt. Berti had no expectations but a slightly larger allowance from her brother, a retired general, on condition she made no contact with the family. 'She's just a remittance woman, that's all she is,' Evelyn frequently remarked. They did not get on well together.

Sisters by a River
Our Spoons Came from Woolworths
Who Was Changed and Who Was Dead
The Vet's Daughter
Out of the Red, into the Blue
The Skin Chairs
Birds in Tiny Cages
A Touch of Mistletoe
*The Juniper Tree
*Mr Fox

BARBARA COMYNS

The House of Dolls

Methuen · Mandarin

A Mandarin Paperback

THE HOUSE OF DOLLS

First published in Great Britain 1989
by Methuen London
This edition published 1990
Reprinted 1990
by Methuen · Mandarin
Michelin House, 81 Fulham Road, London SW3 6RB

Copyright © Barbara Comyns 1989

A CIP catalogue record for this book
is available from the British Library
ISBN 0 7493 0139 2

Printed in Great Britain
by Cox and Wyman Ltd, Reading

I

'Amy Doll, are you telling me that all those old girls upstairs are tarts?'

'Well, not exactly tarts, Doris, but they have gentlemen friends who pay them, you know. It's not very nice, but they say they couldn't manage the rent otherwise. I simply had to put it up, with the expenses rising all the time. You know I never liked that gold and crimson drawing-room although poor Alf thought the world of it, and when he died I thought it would make a nice sitting-room for my ladies; but you should see what they have done with it. It looks real wicked somehow, and they've added to the mirrors and there's a sort of bar, all done up with bamboo, where they serve drinks, at a profit, of course; only, there's always one who drinks behind the others' backs and that causes trouble. It's all very worrying; but there it is. There's little I can do to alter things: they're too strong for me, especially that Berti.'

'What if the police came down on you? Oh, Amy, I can't help laughing when I think how respectable you've always been and now you have turned into a sort of madam. Do they come knocking at the door at all times of the night?' Doris leant back in her chair, her eyes screwed up with laughter and her head lolling on one side. Then she stopped laughing and, opening her eyes very wide, said in a dramatic whisper: 'What about Hetty?'

Amy slowly placed her cup on its saucer and stared at her friend reproachfully. 'As if I haven't thought of that, but what can I do?' she asked. 'She's so fond of the ladies and they have done a lot for her, you must admit; and they wouldn't let her see anything nasty, I'm sure of that. I know they sometimes swear in front of her; but people of that class use dirty language we wouldn't think of using. The Señora doesn't, but she was only a horsemeat butcher until recently. Did I tell you, she's teaching Hetty Spanish and she can "yo tengo" like anything. I wish Alf could hear her. He was so set on her being educated and all that, although I never held with it. Look where it has got them upstairs.'

The two friends sat talking as their tea grew cool and strong. The light that came through the basement window was filtered through the tall stalks of sunflowers growing above. Amy Doll saved their seeds for an elderly gentleman visitor to her ladies, who kept a parrot. They were sitting in what had once been a large kitchen; now, in the Sixties, only the dresser remained and where the old range had been, a proud white Aga water heater stood. The cuckoo came out of the Swiss clock and called five times and Amy briskly jumped to her feet and, collecting cups and saucers and a Lyon's Dundee cake, carried them to the scullery.

Doris reluctantly left her chair; she knew when she was being dismissed. For some time she had sensed that Amy wanted to keep her apart from her daughter. 'Stuck up bitch, and lets her mix with those old pros upstairs,' she muttered behind Amy's neat little back. But she valued the friendship and obediently collected her mauve plastic handbag and arranged her face for the street as she gazed into a pocket looking-glass with violets painted on the back, pouting her lips as she tweaked her hair forward against her plump cheeks. 'Well, I'll be seeing you,' she said as she turned towards the door.

Amy, as if surprised, replied, 'Oh, are you going, dear? I'll see you to the gate.'

They walked through the narrow basement passage together and, as they passed the rusty, dead bells hanging in a row above their heads, Doris observed, as she so often did, 'Christ, those bells give me the pip! Reminds me of when I was a skivvy. They can ring their bells till they are blue in the face, but no one will answer them now.'

Amy glanced at the offending bells and wondered how much it would cost to have them removed, although Alf liked them. 'Being a servant wasn't so bad,' she said. 'We were looked after and had no responsibilities; now it's worry, worry all the time.'

Doris laughed. 'I'll say you've got your worries, all four of them. I say, do you ever have a peep at what's going on, listen at the doors or anything? I'd love to look through their keyholes one night.'

Amy hissed, 'Do hold your tongue, Doris, someone might hear you. Of course I try and ignore the whole thing. I go to bed and listen to old time dancing on my little radio.'

When Doris had gone, she leant over the iron gate in front of her house. As the gentlemen visitors came and went at night it squeaked and banged and she could hear it above the radio, even when she pulled the bedclothes over her head.

Bertha Jago (she called herself Berti) stood at the drawing-room window examining her newly-painted nails. She was a woman of sixty-four, exceptionally tall and bamboo-thin, appearing to have no hips, bottom or breasts. Her skinny knees turned in slightly, as if misshapen from dancing the Charleston too much in her youth. She had small, sad eyes which she opened wide when animated; but in repose her face, below her brilliant red Eton crop, was bitter. This afternoon she was dressed in skin-tight scarlet trews and a crisp white blouse with enormous revers. Berti kept herself scrupulously clean, her clothes always in perfect condition, uncreased and spotless, and her dyed hair glittering with lacquer. Even when drunk she was never dishevelled.

Satisfied that her nails were dry, she crossed the room with her close-knee'd walk and paused in front of the bar. Some years previously a doctor had warned her to cut down on drink and his warning had stayed in her mind. Almost furtively she unlocked the cupboard and took out a whisky bottle, holding it up to the light to see if it had been tampered with. She poured herself a stiff drink, eyed it for a moment, then poured a few drops back into the bottle, which she marked and returned to the cupboard. She kept another bottle in her bedroom which she drank alternately with milk, the milk to line her stomach. She returned to the window, glass in hand. She hated to be alone and even the sight of Amy Doll standing by the gate was reassuring.

Amy's daughter, Hester, came round the corner, swinging her school hat by its elastic and walking as if in a dream. 'She's like a peach,' Berti thought. 'No wonder I want to pinch her.' She watched Amy fuss round the girl, smoothing the long dark hair and adjusting the Alice-band; then take the satchel from her back. Berti waved one long pointed hand; but Hester did not look up. She ran down the basement steps to escape her mother's questions.

The trim figure of Ivy Rope crossed the street. She was the youngest of Amy's ladies — a widow who worked in a haberdashery and woolshop in the nearby Gloucester Road. The pay was small but the work light; it was extremely dull and she often complained in her gentle way; 'I never meet anyone in that stuffy little shop and the knitting wool gets up my nostrils.'

Berti, with her usual impatience, would exclaim, 'If you don't like the work, why don't you do something else?' and Ivy Rope, with tears in her soft grey eyes, would explain how difficult it was for a sheltered woman of fifty, without experience, to get work; how she had once worked in Harrods but it had caused her to have haemorrhoids, and how different it had been when her husband was alive. This usually brought on a fit of weeping and Berti would shout with exasperation, 'Good God, the man's been dead for years! Forget about him.'

This evening, Ivy was smiling to herself. A man was taking her out to dinner. She had met him in a coffee bar and he had only been to the house once. She had managed to rush him up to her small room next to the bathroom without meeting the other tenants and they had sat up there talking and drinking coffee and were only occasionally disturbed by the flushing of the lavatory next door. He obviously had no idea of the kind of house he had been taken to. Then they had made love,

real love, and she hadn't had the heart to spoil everything by asking for money. She did hope he hadn't seen
anything queer on his way downstairs, though. Berti
had a habit of bursting out of her room without a stitch
on and Evelyn wasn't much better with her blouse all
undone. She was proud of her breasts.

As she entered the gate she glanced up and saw Berti
standing at the window and then a beckoning hand,
and knew she was caught. She had hoped to reach her
room unobserved and now she would have to waste
time with the terrifying Berti. As soon as she entered the
hall, Berti rushed at her, exclaiming that she had
something to tell her.

'My dear,' she cried, drawing Ivy into the drawing-
room, 'the most fantastic thing happened to me this
afternoon. I dropped one of my falsies in the bank; you
know, those little rubber things I sometimes wear. A
really charming man picked it up and handed it to me.
I don't think he had any idea what it was I'd dropped,
and when I started to tell him, he just bowed and left
me standing with this thing in my hand and all lopsided.
The strap of my bra had broken. Don't go. Did I ever
tell you about the time the elastic gave in my knickers
at Archie Brook's wedding – second cousin to Sir
George Brook, you know?' Berti usually started her
stories with, 'Did I ever tell you', but never gave her
victim a chance to say, 'Yes, I've heard that story at
least twenty times before.' Ivy patiently let the story run
its course while she debated in her mind whether to
wear her linen suit or the green wild silk. When Berti's
voice ceased for a moment she gave an appreciative
laugh and turned away.

Berti, seeing her audience escaping, caught her by the
arm and, digging her nails into Ivy's flesh, said, 'Wait a

minute, dear, there's still something I want to say to you, I can't remember what. Have a drink while I remember.'

There were footsteps on the stairs and Evelyn Hunter-Smith put her blue-rinsed head round the door. 'Oh, it's you,' she drawled. 'Drinking already? It's only just gone six.' She stood irresolutely by the door and Ivy, slipping past her, hurried up the stairs. She had decided on the green wild silk.

Evelyn Hunter-Smith, a country rector's daughter, was inclined to be a poor man's edition of Berti Jago. They were extraordinarily alike in many ways. Both were divorcees: Berti had been divorced and Evelyn had divorced her husband, who still paid her a small annuity. They were similar in build except that Evelyn was not quite as tall as Berti and she had a bust, which she considered her best feature. Both were addicted to tight trousers and drink and both had cropped heads – only Evelyn's, which had once been dark, was thick and curly. They had small, well-bred faces and rather good noses; but Evelyn's mouth was weak and her teeth inclined to protrude. She was a few years younger than Berti, a fact that she mentioned from time to time. Her annuity from her husband was small, only three hundred a year, but she said she had expectations from an elderly aunt. Berti had no expectations but a slightly larger allowance from her brother, a retired general, on condition she made no contact with the family. 'She's just a remittance woman, that's all she is,' Evelyn frequently remarked. They did not get on well together.

In the garden at the back of the house, Hetty sat among the sunflowers, studying her homework. She found the

French translation easy, the history boring and the maths impossible and decided, as she so often did, to seek help from her so-called 'aunts' upstairs. Her mother would not allow her to enter the upper part of the house after seven in the evening. She bolted the door at the top of the stairs, saying she liked the evenings to be private.

Hetty entered the house by the garden door and found Berti and Evelyn snarling at each other over their drinks. They pounced on her as if she was their saviour, one pouring out Coca-Cola and the other producing a bowl of salted almonds. They were both eager to help with the homework. From experience, Hetty knew that Evelyn was the more reliable, so she handed her her exercise books; then, seeing Berti's disgruntled face, she asked her advice with the French although she knew it would be inaccurate. Fortunately Berti soon lost interest and started telling one of the many adventures of her youth, which Hetty had heard before, but she smiled and nibbled her nuts. She was a good listener.

The gate groaned and clanked and both the 'aunts' rushed to the window. 'Oh, it's for you,' Evelyn sighed. 'It's that unpleasant little man with the red eyes.'

Berti patted her sleek hair before one of the ornate mirrors. 'Poor Jim Clarke! He used to own a string of race horses and gave the most marvellous week-end parties. I met him first in Hong Kong, before my marriage broke up. Let him in, Hetty dear.'

Hetty went slowly to the door. She knew poor old Jim Clarke from before and his watering, inflamed eyes disgusted her. She opened the door and he tottered in.

'Well, young lady, it isn't often I have the pleasure of seeing you,' he wheezed and made as if to kiss her. She laughed as she moved away. The aunts' visitors often tried to kiss her and she had become an expert at avoiding them.

'Ah, Berti, my dear,' and the old faces were pressed together for a moment before Berti helped him to a chair. 'I can only stay a few minutes,' he said as he adjusted his hearing aid. 'My son, Frank, and his wife are visiting me this evening and they'll have me in bed by nine o'clock – no drinks, of course; they treat me as if I were in my dotage. Pour me out a quick one, Berti dear. I have some tablets here, for the breath you know, for the breath. Ah, Evelyn, I didn't see you sitting over there, busy with your accounts. You are looking very lovely with your blue hair.'

Evelyn picked up the books. 'It's only this child's homework,' she said coldly. 'I think we'll finish it downstairs, Hetty.'

Hetty agreed. She was glad to leave the room and Jim Clarke. She was expecting him to fall back dead in his chair in front of her eyes. 'If he didn't take those tablets, would he die, Aunt Evelyn?' she asked as they went down the basement stairs. 'Don't tell Mother I let him in. She doesn't like me to meet these old men who come to the house. I suppose you have them because they're so old and lonely and you cheer them up.'

Amy was ironing and her heart sank when Evelyn followed her daughter into the room. With the slightest encouragement Evelyn would spend hours in the basement talking about her previous life, her aristocratic family and present worries – Berti in particular. She often came down on the pretext of helping Amy, which meant at the most shelling a few peas or making one of her special fruit salads. These involved opening at least four expensive tins of fruit and cutting the contents into tiny squares.

'I can't think why you can't do your homework on your own without bothering your aunts,' she said crossly, and added to Evelyn, 'she stayed away from school twice last week and I can't get out of her where she spent the time. In a garden, she says. It's lucky the school inspector doesn't come after her or there'd be another scandal on my hands.' The angry smell of scorched linen filled the room. 'There, now I've scorched a pillow-case, and they don't grow on trees.'

Evelyn peered at the scorched linen with her large, myopic eyes: 'Never mind, put it on my pillow. Perhaps it'll wash out the next time you take it to the laundrette. I always think you iron so beautifully, Mrs Doll. I know Berti doesn't agree with me and says that you iron the sheets folded so that they have lines running all over them, but you know what she is. Now I've upset your bowl of water. Oh, dear, let me fill it for you.'

There was a knock at the door and a large smooth face topped by jet-black hair appeared round the door. 'There's a gentleman asking for you, Mrs Evelyn.'

'Who is it, Señora? Do I know him?'

'I've seen him before but I don't know his name. He's a very small gentleman.'

'Then it must be Harry Rutter. I know he's small, but so amusing and very well connected. I must run. Shall I take the pillow-case up to my room, Mrs Doll?'

'No, leave it,' Amy answered coldly. 'I'll see what a little bleach will do.'

The two women left the room and Amy and Hetty were alone. 'I'll just run upstairs and bolt the door, then we'll be private,' Amy said as she laid down her iron, 'and turn on the wireless; we could do with a little music.'

* * *

The Señora, as they called her, was in fact a señorita, in spite of her matronly figure. Augustina Puig had been living in the Dolls' house for over eight years. She came shortly after Alf Doll had bought the house and, until his death two years later, she had been the only tenant. He had left nothing except the house and his small but growing builder's business in the Fulham Road. 'Just a builder's yard and a few ladders, buckets and brushes,' the man who offered to buy the business said; but Augustina Puig saw that he gave the widow something for the good will and eventually Amy received over a thousand pounds which she invested in a building society. Although Amy Doll was eternally grateful to her Spanish lodger for her help, the two women never became intimate and they were still 'Mrs Doll' and 'Señora Puig' to each other. Amy had never enquired what this magnificent Spanish woman was doing in a Walham Green horsemeat shop or wondered how she came to leave her country. She was just Augustina Puig, whom her husband had brought home one evening when he was engaged in decorating the horsemeat shop.

'She'd fit nicely into the big room at the top,' he said, 'and the money she brings will pay for Hetty's schooling.' And later, 'It's a pleasure to see her coming and going. I'll bet she wears corsets, the old-fashioned kind, all whalebone and laces.'

Augustina's parents had been Barcelona butchers and as a girl she had worked in the butcher's shop helping her mother to chop up the carcasses of animals and eventually being allowed to cut fillets of beef at the counter. But they were a large family and she had been sent away to work as a servant at a rich customer's house. Besides training her, her mistress had taught her to read and write and things had gone well until the morning the señor had followed her into his wife's bedroom and tried to rape her. Her screams had brought the entire household clamouring to the door which the señor calmly opened and walked away from as if it had nothing to do with him. The señora immediately dismissed the girl and she was sent home in disgrace. Her family never forgave her.

She was sent to Sitges to work as a chambermaid in a hotel owned by Germans and, although she sent most of her wages home to her family, she was treated as an outcast. When she occasionally went home her mother's sighs echoed round the meat and her younger sisters giggled together. She continued to send money home until her mother's death ten years later.

Augustina was not happy working in a hotel and returned to private service and eventually found work with a retired British major who owned a villa at Sitges. She was a beautiful girl and after a few weeks he persuaded her to become his mistress. They lived together very happily for a number of years until the major's health began to decline, then he returned to England bringing Augustina with him, and they settled in Brighton. Then he died, leaving her a few hundred pounds. It had seemed a vast sum to her at the time; but it soon began to melt away and she had to find work, at first as a Brighton waitress, where she was overworked and unhappy, then in London at an Italian restaurant, where she was overworked but happy, until it was destroyed by incendiary bombs during the war. She would always remember the horror of arriving one morning to find the burnt and smouldering remains of the restaurant where she had been working a few hours previously, the charred black skeletons of the chairs still standing at the twisted iron tables with their cracked marble tops, the tarnished till and the stained walls. Most of the ceiling had been burnt away and she could see the wrecked rooms above. It appeared to have been that way for an eternity, completely dead. After the shock she longed for the comfort of meat. She wanted to work surrounded by great lumps of it. The labour exchange directed her to the horsemeat shop and, although the meat was inferior, she found it comforting.

When she came to live with the Dolls in Mulberry Grove she was already the mistress of a chocolate salesman who gave her a constant supply of chocolates and an allowance and, when she retired from the horsemeat shop, she took another lover and, with Amy's reluctant permission, brought him home twice a week. From that, it was only a step to what she called 'my casual gentlemen'. In their early days at Mulberry Grove, both Berti and Evelyn had occasionally allowed a man friend to stay the night; but they were united in fury when they discovered what was going on.

When they taxed the Señora with her immoral behaviour she calmly advised them to follow her example: 'Our landlady has been forced to put up the rents of our rooms by the rising cost of living – and it isn't only the rent: the gas meters have been reset. And have you noticed the price of transport and cigarettes? I don't smoke myself, but how are you ladies going to manage? There is always a cigarette in your hands, and drink, you are very fond of drink, both of you. How will you manage? I think you have parted with most of your jewellery as it is.' This was true, but how did the Señora know?

Her listeners exchanged glances, then Berti asked in an unusually hesitant voice, 'Er, well, how much do you charge your "casual gentlemen"?'

The Señora pursed her lips. 'It depends on the sort of gentlemen they are. I go by their clothes, chiefly, particularly their shirts. A man with a frayed collar or soiled shirt is no use at all. I choose very carefully. Of course, at our sort of age one can't charge too much, two or three pounds at the most. It's the regulars that make it worth while. I suppose I earn an average of seventeen pounds a week, no tax, of course; I could earn more if I weren't so particular.' She paused, then added, 'I think being foreign is an added attraction. I usually pretend my English isn't very good.'

'Where do you meet these men?' Berti asked. She was beginning to enjoy herself. Evelyn's usually pale face was flushed and although she was listening intently, she hummed a little tune to herself, taking no part in the conversation.

'I mean, you don't just pick them up in the street. Do you advertise on those boards?'

'Certainly not. Nothing like that,' the Señora replied indignantly. 'I sometimes take a coffee at a station waiting-room. There's a good deal of coming and going at that sort of place. And then there are wine clubs. Many solitary men like a glass of wine now and then. I mostly rely on wine clubs. I think the coffee bars would suit you two ladies — and the museums on wet afternoons.'

'Two ladies?' Evelyn asked icily.

'Come off it, Evelyn. You know you are as interested as I am,' Berti snapped. 'We could turn this room into a sort of saloon. I know Jim Clarke would adore to come. It'd remind him of old times. And there's Freddy Gore. He's always complaining about how dull life is these days. My God! What about our modest violet — Ivy Rope?'

The Señora smiled with confidence. 'I think she will come in with us. She's very fond of dress, that one, and lonely too. She'll protest, of course, but she'll join us.'

The Señora was right. Ivy was shocked to the marrow. The name of the dead Mr Rope was added to the protests, the lacy handkerchiefs she bought at a discount from the haberdasher's were soaked with tears; then she turned on Berti: 'It's all very well for you,' she sobbed. 'You've lived a bad life and already have two men friends. I've hardly spoken to a man since my husband died and now you want to turn me into a p-p-prostitute.'

Berti laughed. 'Well, there's no need for you to join us if you feel so badly about it; we'll just go ahead. I think we need a few more gilt mirrors, don't you, Evelyn? I noticed some Victorian ones in a shop in the Fulham Road, amazingly cheap really. Later on, we could buy some small gilt tables. Oh, and a bar. We must have a bar and nude statues if they're not too expensive. Perhaps dear old Jim could give us a few hints on how the room should be furnished.'

Ivy cried, 'I see how it is, you want to shut me out! After all, it's partly my drawing-room and I'm younger than all of you and more attractive in my quiet way. Men often follow me in the street, but of course, I always hurry on.'

Eventually the Señora took her in hand, introducing her to a chiropodist who lived a lonely life with a frigid wife in north London. The chiropodist and Ivy got on beautifully, but unfortunately he could only afford fifteen shillings a visit. She also collected a cynical widower in an Earl's Court coffee bar; although she did not like him, for a time she had hopes that he might marry her, but it turned out he lived with a sister who looked after him very well. It amused him to sit in the red and gold drawing-room drinking and talking to his hostesses, especially Berti, but it was always Ivy he went upstairs with. Berti had two elderly admirers, Jim Clarke and Freddy Gore. The difficulty was collecting new ones. She tried sitting in coffee bars and the saloons of public houses with what she called a 'come-hither' expression on her face, without much success. Sometimes men followed her when she left; then it turned out it was girls they were after and they had mistaken her for a procuress. She did manage to add one more old man to her collection, who paid her two pounds a week for the pleasure of sitting in the wicked drawing-room, drinking and hearing risqué conversation. He never ventured upstairs.

Evelyn did not manage so well. She used to haunt bars and make out she was waiting for someone, standing nervously near the door when it became clear that she had been let down by her friend. She would hesitantly ask the barman if he had seen a tall man with grey hair wearing a dark suit; 'You see, I'm a little late and we'd arranged to meet at seven and now it's nearly half-past.' She'd take one last look among the drinkers, then make slowly to the door.

Occasionally someone, seeing her distressed, aristocratic profile, would offer her a drink, which gave her the opportunity to entice them back to the house in Mulberry Grove. She failed to make it quite clear what Mulberry Grove had to offer, but she sometimes aroused their curiosity. When she did manage to bring them back with her, they sat in the ornate drawing-room, drinking and laughing their heads off. 'This is fantastic, it really is.' If encouraged, Berti would shed her clothes and leap about the room on her skinny legs, dancing the dances of her youth. Although they only came to laugh and drink, they usually left something substantial on one of the little tables and sometimes returned with their friends.

The Señora did not use the drawing-room much, and when she did, her presence had a restraining influence. Although well advanced in middle-age, she was the only one who managed to bring back young men. It happened very seldom, and when it did she refused to take any money, although she was saving hard. She had had no 'novio' when she was young and felt she had missed something.

2

When Amy had confided to her friend Doris that her house was being used as a brothel for elderly gentle-people, her fears of the house being raided were gradually fading. It had been going on for two years and the only time she felt really worried was when a policeman passed through Mulberry Grove, particularly if he turned his head towards her front garden. Now a new fear had been added to her troubled mind; Hetty's headmistress had sent for Amy and interviewed her in her forbidding study. She complained that the child was absent from school at least two days a week, besides being invariably bottom of her class. Her homework was better than her classwork and the headmistress looked reproachfully at Amy as if accusing her of doing Hetty's homework. She took a mild interest in languages, but otherwise gave no attention to her lessons; in fact, she was so backward they were beginning to think she was mentally retarded.

'Mentally retarded?' Amy quavered. 'Do you mean a bit soft in the head? Oh, I know she's vague and dreamy, but there's nothing really wrong. I mean, she can learn if she wants to. You should hear her doing the old "yo tengo" with the Señora. We have a Spanish lady living in the house.' Then sadly, 'I suppose you're right, the child's not quite normal, always in a dream. Couldn't walk until she was two, just sat in her pram, thinking. Very quiet she was, couldn't talk either. But she's a happy child and lovely to look at, you must admit.'

The headmistress agreed, but added that she was not interested in girls' appearances as long as they were clean and neat. Actually Hetty would have been sent away from the school years ago if her looks had not been such an asset. Visitors always noticed the beautiful girl with the long dark hair and she was a great attraction in the school plays. This autumn term she was to be the Madonna in the Nativity play.

Eventually it was arranged that Amy would bring her daughter to school in the mornings and the interview ended. 'A great girl of nearly fourteen: it's a disgrace,' she muttered as she left the school. 'This is what happens when a girl's educated above her station; but I can't bring myself to go against Alf's wishes, poor man, lying all cold in Brompton Cemetery.'

If Hetty resented her mother accompanying her to school each morning, she said little. They sat together in the 49 bus, Hetty gazing out at the London streets and her mother fretting in her mind over the household chores she could be doing at home and here she was, wasting time on a bus. She enjoyed passing through Kensington High Street, exclaiming from time to time, 'Look! Barkers have changed their window again,' or, 'They've still got that blue coat in C & A's window. I wish I could see the price from here.' They left the bus at Holland Park and, if Hetty was joined by school friends, Amy scuttled off home. One morning, she overheard one of the girls ask if she was the maid.

'She won't play truant now she's with her friends, she'll go along with them.' Amy was mistaken. Hetty still stayed away from school, but not so frequently.

She had been perfectly truthful with her mother when she told her that she stayed away from school so that she could spend her time in a garden. It belonged to a derelict house skulking behind house agents' boards in Holland Villas Road. With its broken windows and dismal front garden, it looked a forbidding place; but she had discovered a laurel-enclosed side entrance which led to a surprisingly large garden with a long, over-grown lawn and a summer-house sheltered by lime trees. She amused herself by clearing one of the flower-beds and making a mosaic with pieces of broken glass, china and stones. It was supposed to represent Christ with a lamb on his shoulder. The halo, a broken yellow plate, she considered particularly successful and she was pleased with his hair and beard of glistening crushed coal. But the lamb was giving trouble; what ever she did with it, it continued to look like a bundle of dripping laundry. A stray cat had had kittens in the summer-house and food from home had to be smuggled to them, stolen tins of sardines and scraps salvaged from the dustbin, dry cheese, fish heads; they ate anything.

Then a man who had once lived in the house appeared and she made a friend of him. He was a large, shambling creature with a pair of huge leather gloves sewn to a tape hanging from each shoulder like extra hands. He must have been over fifty, but his mind had stayed around twelve. She called him Glover and never learnt his real name. He joined in the mosaic work with enthusiasm, spending weeks composing a swan swim-ming on a bottle-green glass river, wearing his gloves as he worked with the glass to protect his hands. He liked to talk about his young days when he lived in the house with his family as he did so: 'You see the window at the top with the bars, that was our nursery, and, if you come to the front, I'll show you the room where I was born; my sister and I were both born there, but they say I came feet first, that's unusual, you know. The school-room was at the back, with steps leading into the garden, and in summer we drank our morning glass of milk sitting on the steps.'

He showed her faded photographs of family tea-parties in front of the summer-house and one of himself dressed in a sailor suit with a croquet mallet in his hand. This gave him the idea that the croquet set might still be in the house and one day she came to find him on his knees, cutting the rough grass with a pair of shears, and a long, dirty box containing the croquet set in the summer-house. They took turns to cut the grass and found working with shears tired them and using scissors made blisters come on their hands. The lawn was not very smooth when they decided it was finished, but they felt a great sense of achievement as they hammered the croquet hoops into position. Constructing mosaics and playing croquet kept them happy until well into October. Then Glover caught a cold which went to his chest and decided it was time the croquet set was put away. The cat with its kittens had already left and the autumn garden lost its charm.

'We'll meet in the spring,' Glover croaked between fits of coughing. 'They are taking me to the South of France. Can't bear the place, but they said I must go. I've a new idea for a mosaic – a golden chalice made of pebbles wrapped in coloured toffee papers against a background of blue china. You'll look out for blue china while I'm away, won't you, Hester?' They parted without regret, as children do. They'd meet again in the spring

Hetty's fourteenth birthday was due at the end of October. Each time a birthday came round she asked for a dog, a cat or a bicycle in that order; but Amy didn't want the basement cluttered up with animals and she considered a bicycle dangerous in London. This year she had reluctantly agreed to an aquarium, and as a birthday treat it had been arranged that Evelyn would take Hetty and three friends to the theatre. After a lot of discussion, *Oliver* had been chosen. Amy felt she couldn't face taking the children herself: she didn't want to be taken for a servant and let the poor child down.

Two years ago the aunts upstairs had given a birthday party for her. At Amy's suggestion, the drawing-room had had some of the wickedness taken away and the aunts dressed discreetly, Berti and Evelyn wearing skirts. Amy had made a huge pink and white birthday cake, but everything else had been provided by her tenants. They had hired a conjuror and provided an unusual tea consisting of Danish open sandwiches, canapés and a vast meringue filled with ice-cream. The food was a great success with the children and only after they had gone home was it noticed how much had been stamped into the carpet. The only mishap occurred at the end of the party when the parents came to collect their children. Berti, who had been behaving beautifully, answered the door to a particularly handsome and distinguished father and took him straight up to her room, and it was a few minutes before he realized what her intentions were. As he hurried down the stairs, green in the face with shocked disgust, he bumped into Evelyn, who exclaimed, 'The underhand bitch! Did she take you to her room? Come to the drawing-room and I'll give you a drink.' She slipped her arm into his and drew him into the hall.

He shook her off and snarled, 'All I want is my daughter. She must leave this house immediately.'

Fortunately Amy appeared in the hall looking as wholesome and pure as a milkmaid. She showed him into the drawing-room, where his daughter was saying goodbye to some friends. There were several respectable parents standing about, trying to persuade their children to leave. In spite of the rather gaudy furniture it all appeared normal enough. He left the house a shaken and bewildered man.

Although Hetty was tall for her age, she was young mentally. At fourteen, most of her contempories at school were interested in pop singers and film stars; they nearly all owned transistors and used make-up at weekends. They talked about boys and, if they had brothers at school, they wrote to their friends even if they'd never met them. The important thing was to receive a letter from a boy which could be shown round the class. These things meant nothing to Hetty, whose idea of heaven was to spend Saturday morning in Harrods' pet department or wandering round the South Kensington museums. Her favourite reading was a collection of bound old *Punches* and *Girl's Owns* her father had bought in a sale years ago. She was beginning to take an interest in dress and sometimes studied Ivy Rope's fashion magazines and liked to look through her wardrobe. She said her prayers every night and inevitably ended with, 'And, please, God, can I have a hen?' She no longer wished for a hen, but had ended her prayers that way for nearly ten years.

Her fourteenth birthday came on a Saturday and the aunts came down together with their gifts and to see the aquarium which contained tropical fish and was illuminated. It seemed to Hetty the most beautiful thing she had ever seen, with the jewel-like fish darting between the shells and delicate water plants. Evelyn gave her a coral-coloured lipstick, the first Hetty had owned and frowned on by Amy. There were nylon stockings from Ivy, the Señora had embroidered fine handkerchiefs with her initials, and Berti, who always liked to outdo the other aunts, had given her a Victorian silver-backed mirror. It was exactly the kind of thing that appealed to Hetty and it was obvious that she preferred it to the other presents, which was precisely what Berti had hoped would happen. In point of fact, Hetty was out of favour with her because of a tactless remark she had made a few days previously. Wandering vaguely round the drawing-room, she had asked, 'When do people turn into folk, old folk, you know. Are all of you people or have you become folk?'

'Really, Hester dear,' Ivy said reproachfully, 'I'm only fifty-one, a comparatively young woman.'

'Depends on who you are compared with,' Evelyn drawled, then, turning to Hetty, said, 'It's very rude to make remarks like that. You must think before you speak.'

'But I was thinking. I've thought about it quite a lot. I'm sorry if I said something I shouldn't.'

Berti, who had been smouldering over her glass of whisky, suddenly snapped, 'Damn you, you impertinent little fool! Go down to your basement.' Hetty went.

The Señora, who had not quite gathered what was happening, cried, '*Que pasa? Que pasa?*' She only spoke in Spanish when she was disturbed.

3

When the short damp days of November came, the sound of the Thames barges hooting to each other floated over the acid air and Amy scrubbed falling soot from the painted window-sills. Now, the elderly gentlemen visitors didn't ring the front-door bell so frequently. They stayed at home and nursed their bronchitis and sometimes there were evenings when no one came at all and Berti and Evelyn sat upstairs drinking and quarrelling.

Ivy Rope went out with her new friend twice a week and returned in the early hours of the morning, often not returning at all on Saturday nights. She never risked bringing her lover to Mulberry Grove after the first time because she knew that Berti and Evelyn were consumed with curiosity, questioning her without mercy. They asked why she didn't bring him to the house and how much money he was paying her. They were particularly interested in the amount she was getting. Poor Ivy, who had never mentioned money to her lover, mumbled something about pounds.

'Extra if you stay the night, I presume,' Berti said, fixing her tinted bifocals on Ivy's shrinking face. 'Two pounds twice a week. Why, you'll be in my income group soon. What is his home like? Is he married, divorced or another of your widowers?'

Ivy, backing towards the door, told her he was divorced. 'He unfortunately married a woman much younger than himself and it didn't last.'

'How old is he, for Heaven's sake?' Evelyn demanded. 'Eighty?'

'No, of course not. His isn't fifty yet.'

Berti smiled. 'I see, younger than you, then. Oh, don't go.' Ivy reached the door and was fiddling with the cut-glass handle. 'You haven't told us what he does yet. I mean, what does he do for a living?'

'I'm afraid I don't know,' Ivy squeaked, as she made a bolt for the downstairs lavatory.

'We can't very well follow her,' Berti said reluctantly. 'I'm sure there's something fishy about that man's profession. Perhaps he's a fishmonger.' They laughed together in harmony for once.

'I shouldn't be surprised if he didn't have a fish and chip stall,' Evelyn said spitefully, 'and that is why she doesn't want us to see him. You know how sensitive she is.'

'Yes, that's it. He's connected with fish,' Berti agreed. 'I know, we'll ask her if she's eaten any good haddock lately and see if she bolts for the loo again.'

They sat over their drinks and made a show of listening to each other.

'I can remember our old butler, now what was his name? Ah, Maltravers. Well, Maltravers was a great character and he always said . . .' Berti rambled on, sipping her stomach-lining glass of milk.

Evelyn, fumbling for a cigarette, said dreamily, 'And the groom used to bring the horses round every morning for us to ride. We had two hunters called, now let me see, Thunder and Lightning, that's what they were called. I expect I've told you about this aunt who lived with us and adored me, the one who is leaving me all her money,' she boasted, swaying slightly in her chair. 'And the peacocks on the lawn. There were four of them, all waving their gorgeous tails.'

Berti sighed. 'Yes, dear, I've heard all that before. What about another whisk? There's still some left in the bottle.'

They sat in dreamy silence over their drinks. The half-forgotten face of her little dead sister passed through Berti's memories. She had died of meningitis and the servants said her eyes went blood-red; but Berti remembered them large and blue under a sun hat as the two girls raked their garden plots. They had lived in Hertfordshire and their father had gone to London every day, driven to the station by the gardener-handyman in an open trap drawn by a cob with a docked tail. What happened when it rained? she wondered, and a vague memory of sitting under a giant umbrella and the sound of rain and horses hooves flitted across her mind. Then she was playing in a neglected part of the village churchyard with the vicar's son, a white-faced boy called Patrick. The long nettles stung their legs and while they searched for a dock leaf the boy had suddenly unbuttoned his trousers and said, 'I'll show you my penis if you'll show me your bosoms.' She laughed and disturbed Evelyn, who was asleep and dreaming of the South of France where she had lived for some years after her divorce. She looked at Berti reproachfully. It had been a happy dream.

'You've given me too much to drink,' she said,

yawning. 'I'll feel it tomorrow. Perhaps some food would help. What about opening a tin of baked beans?'

Amy sat below, waiting for 'The Archers'. She had already had a session with 'The Dales'. She sometimes wondered what all those good people would think of her household; she felt she was letting them down. As 'The Archers' signature tune pealed out of the plastic wireless, there was a ring at the back door bell. She sadly left her comfortable chair and went to answer it, only opening the door a chink in case it was someone with a gun. She almost collapsed when she saw a policeman standing there with a piece of paper in his hand. 'It's all up,' she thought. 'Will it be prison or a fine? Whichever happens, my name will be in the papers with an identikit photograph perhaps and oh, my God, they'll put Hetty in care and protection.'

The policeman said, 'Good evening,' quite pleasantly. There was nothing threatening in his manner as he asked, 'Is there a Margaret Mumpford living here?'

Amy shook her trim head. 'No, there's no one of that name in the house,' she whispered.

'You're sure?' the policeman asked. 'No Margaret Mumpford who was sent off to a private hospital recently, in point of fact, a mental home? She's missing and this is the address she gave.'

Amy gave the policeman a penetrating look. Perhaps there really was a mistake and she had nothing to worry about. 'Oh no,' she said firmly, 'there's no one like that here. My four ladies are all in the house and none of them have been away for years. They're not mental or anything like that, just eccentric, that's all, inspector.'

'None of them are called Mumpford, then?'

'There's no one of that name and never has been,'

Amy snapped and made to shut the door. She didn't like the way the policeman stared. Eventually he clumped away in his heavy shoes, a threat in every step. She returned to the sitting-room and switched off the wireless. 'The Archers' had finished and from Hetty's bedroom she could hear her reading to the Señora in Spanish and felt a surge of pride. Whatever happened, no one could say the child's education had been neglected.

Three days later the policeman was standing on Amy's doorstep again, this time in broad daylight. He said he had come to apologize for disturbing her the other evening. He had found the missing Margaret Mumpford in a house a little further down the road; she had given a false address. 'Well, that settles it,' Amy said brightly.

But instead of going the policeman started asking questions: 'Just a moment, forgive me for asking, but is this house in your husband's name?'

Amy, with a stricken look, muttered something about her husband being dead for over six years and that the house was in her name. She longed to add, 'And what is that to do with you?' but dared not speak rudely to the law.

'I'm sorry to bother you with these questions, Mrs . . . ? I don't think I know your name.'

Amy faltered, 'It's Doll, Amy Doll.'

'Amy Doll', he repeated as if he enjoyed the name. Then he turned away. 'Good morning, Mrs Doll. Sorry to have bothered you.' And, smiling, he went away.

Poor Amy returned to the kitchen. There was a delicious smell of fried liver and onions, but she hadn't the heart to eat. She sadly said to herself, 'I suppose he's what they call playing cat and mouse with me. It's a pity such a nice-looking man can be so cruel.'

4

On Sundays Berti and Evelyn both wore skirts. They hung round the telephone in the hope that someone would invite them to lunch. If no invitation materialized by twelve, Evelyn would buy a bottle of cheap wine at the off-licence and call on her few friends. On the last Sunday of every month she had a standing invitation to visit some cousins who lived at Twickenham. She was never made welcome there, but it was somewhere to go and she could boast about her cousin's large house and garden on her return. Occasionally, Harry Rutter would take her to an 'amusing little restaurant' he had discovered. The amusing little restaurant inevitably turned out to be a dirty little place in some dreary back street that served greasy food. When she came home she told Berti and Ivy that she had eaten the most marvellous meal at an exclusive little restaurant Harry had found. She had promised not to reveal where it was. Harry was an absolute epicure.

'A self-service Lyon's in Kilburn most likely,' Berti would sniff.

Even with the odd greasy meal eaten in Harry Rutter's company, there were a great many Sundays left on

Evelyn's hands and the bottle of wine came in useful. She would call on the few people she had managed to scrape up an acquaintance with, brandishing her bottle, in the hope they would ask her to lunch. If her first visit failed, she would go off with her bottle and call on someone else, usually just as they were about to serve luncheon, and get into the kitchen and offer to help. Although the husbands ground their teeth in the background, the wives were often forced to give some sort of invitation and in a moment she was laying an extra place for herself and demanding wine-glasses for her contribution to the meal.

Sundays were no problem to Ivy now. She spent them in Putney with her dentist lover and they would often cook a meal together or he would drive her into the country. It was years since she had been so happy. The much-lamented Mr Rope had been a selfish old man who had spent most of his time at his club, eating enormous meals there and keeping his wife short of housekeeping money. He was years older than her, but instead of being an old man's darling she had been his slave. When he died, it turned out that he had bought himself a handsome annuity which had died with him and Ivy was left with nothing except a few pieces of ugly furniture and the tail-end of a lease, which she sold for a hundred pounds and out of which she had to pay for her husband's funeral.

Nevertheless, Mr Rope's failings were now forgotten and his widow thought up new virtues for him every day. The only thing he had given her was a false security and comparative freedom from responsibility. She found managing on her own a terrifying experience and she was constantly searching for someone to take care of her. Now she had a lover, but how to turn him into a husband she didn't know. He was several years younger than she was and she was sure that if he knew about her life at the house in Mulberry Grove he would have no more to do with her. All the same, she still lived in hope and smiled at her customers as she served them with skeins of wool and embroidery silks.

With envy, Berti and Evelyn watched Ivy tripping down the front-steps in her high-heeled shoes. She was wearing a new grey coat and skirt and her pretty soft hair had been rinsed a champagne colour. 'Spends everything on her back,' Evelyn said, tearing herself away from the vicinity of the telephone and staring through the window. 'She says he took her to Maidenhead and they lunched at Skindles.'

'Skindles,' Berti shrugged scornfully, 'it's nothing to what it was. Did I ever tell you about the time Tom Lawrence threw me into the river from Skindles' lawn? He was always pestering me to marry him and I refused once too often and he suddenly went crazy.'

'Must have been if he wanted to marry you.' Evelyn laughed.

'Christ! How you bore me with your schoolgirl humour. I say, did you notice the colour of her hair? She's not a bad-looking little thing in her way. No sex appeal, of course.'

Evelyn agreed. 'I've mentioned fish to her several times, but had no reaction.'

'So've I. We must be on the wrong track. But I'm sure there's something wrong with him, or why is she so secretive?'

The telephone rang. Berti managed to reach it first and sharply slapped Evelyn's outstretched hand. 'You wish to speak to Señora Puig?' she cooed. 'I'm afraid she's out. She's seldom here on Sundays, but could I help in any way?' The only reply was a sharp click. 'Surly bugger, he's replaced the receiver,' Berti said crossly, frowning at the telephone.

Evelyn smiled and looked at her watch. 'Heavens!' she giggled. 'I've just remembered, some friends are expecting me for luncheon. I must fly!' She flew to the off-licence in Old Brompton Road to buy a bottle of cheap Spanish wine. Berti, still frowning, waited by the telephone; but it remained silent.

Down in the basement Amy Doll was basting the Sunday joint, a nice leg of lamb surrounded by roasting potatoes. She was expecting Doris for lunch and was hoping that she wouldn't bring her illegitimate son with her — a hulking boy with furry cheeks. He had been conceived when Amy and Doris worked together at the big house in the Boltons, his father being the bread roundsman, who took to delivering bread in another district when he heard about Doris's condition. When it became apparent, Doris was returned to her mother in Walham Green, 'like a bitch in whelp,' her old mother said with bitterness. When the baby was born Doris called him Solomon because she thought his father might have been a Jew and it was a good biblical name for a poor illegitimate boy. She never returned to private service, but made a good living as a waitress in a city restaurant. The men tipped her well because they liked her cheeky backchat; they were all friendly, some more than friendly. Doris enjoyed the life.

The hulking son was now nearly sixteen, a clever boy who did well at school. He was of a singularly unattractive appearance which belied his kindly nature. Amy always thought of the poor boy as 'a limb of Satan' because he had been conceived in sin and she shivered when he came near Hetty. Sometimes he brought his bicycle to the house and allowed her to ride it round the square, in spite of Amy's protests. He was devoted to Hetty, and Doris sometimes said, 'Wouldn't it be nice if they made a match of it?' Amy frowned and refused to reply to such an unwelcome suggestion. The cheek of it!

Sure enough, this Sunday Solly came thudding down the steps after his mother and immediately asked for Hetty.

'I'm here, Sol,' she called from her bedroom. 'Come and see my aquarium.'

Amy darted from the kitchen. 'What a thing to do, asking boys into your bedroom!' she cried; but Solly was already with Hetty and Doris said, 'Oh, leave the kids alone, they like to be together.'

There was a knock at the door and Berti slithered in, wearing a narrow black skirt. 'My dear,' she asked, 'I suppose you couldn't spare me a little of your meal; it smells delicious. I'd arranged to lunch with friends, but this wretched toothache came on and I really don't feel up to it. Could I just have a bite with you?'

Amy said she was welcome to a meal but she would have to have it upstairs: 'You see, there's the four of us and that little round table won't take any more. No, I'll bring you something upstairs at about one, Miss Berti, and, when you've finished, leave the tray outside the door and I'll send Hetty up for it.' Amy wasn't going to put up with Berti and Doris swapping dirty stories in the kitchen; as it was, Doris was looking at her in an unnerving way. It was the first time she had seen her since Amy had told her about the goings-on upstairs.

Berti loved to be noticed. 'I see you're looking at my skirt. I only wear them on Sundays because I hate the bloody things, but one must conform a little, I suppose.

My God!' She held a pointed hand to her withered cheek. A sliver of pain ran from a tooth and up her startled face, ending in the cheekbone; then it appeared to slowly creep back into the tooth, curl up and remain a dull ache. Toothache had really come. Amy produced a bottle of aspirins and Doris gave advice about dentists.

'I suppose you are registered with one round here, but I've found a smasher in Putney. He's so gentle and hardly hurts at all. It's worth the journey. Anyway, I'll write down the name and address for you.' Berti took the piece of paper with her when she left the room to make a bee line for the drink cupboard. She hoped a mouthful of neat whisky might deaden the pain.

Quivering with misery, she drank her whisky, between sips running her tongue round the offending tooth. She wondered if it was a punishment for telling lies on Sunday. Berti couldn't bear pain and the thought of a session in a dentist's chair terrified her. Some years ago she had been to a dentist who had extracted three teeth and had made an appointment, which she did not keep, to extract two more. 'I could have sat at the side table,' she thought miserably, 'but they didn't want me downstairs. Of course, the reason may have been that they felt too embarrassed to sit down at table with someone of a different class. Yes, I expect that was it.' The drink was beginning to work. 'How is it that I have lost touch with them all? There was Roley, I've forgotten his other name – it may have begun with a J. We had such fun together. I wonder what became of him. If I could remember his surname I could look him up in the telephone book. I'll make a list of old friends' names, ones I haven't quarrelled with, and see if I can find them in the directory.'

After an idyllic day in Putney, Ivy came home to find

Berti with a brilliant headsquare draped round her face, curled up on the drawing-room sofa. The carved gilt table in front of her was littered with glasses of whisky, milk, aspirins, a pile of telephone directories and a scribbled list of names decorated with question marks and crosses.

'Ivy, dear,' Berti said in the slurred voice that meant she had been drinking, 'I've had the most frightful day. I should have lunched with the Cromptons, cousins of the old Viceroy, but this devastating toothache came on and I haven't stirred at all. Do sit down and have a drink. It's from my private bottle and won't cost you anything. I must tell you what I've been doing. Looking up old friends in the telephone book. Naturally I have forgotten half their names and must admit I've quarrelled with quite a few, but eventually I found the name of Henn; I couldn't forget that, could I? Henn-Crosby, only we always called him Cocky. He had a villa in Corfu the year I was there and gave the most fabulous parties. At one, I remember, there were a couple of lesbians performing right in the middle of the floor and, at another, the women guests all went nude to the waist and the men nude below the waist. Of course, all his parties weren't like that. Some of them were very starchy; friends arriving in yachts and all that sort of thing. Heavens, you do look queer! Have I shocked you?' Ivy's eyes were riveted to a piece of torn paper lying among the litter on the table.

'What is this doing here? Is it for me?' Her voice quavered and her hand went towards the paper.

Berti snatched it away. 'Oh, that! It is the address of a dentist a friend of Amy's gave me. I'll get in touch with him tomorrow if I'm still in pain. It seems a long way to go; somewhere near Putney Bridge, she said.'

'Putney, why, that's miles away. There's a very good man near my shop, all the customers swear by him. If you like I'll make an appointment with him tomorrow. You can't go to an unknown man in Putney, his instruments may be crawling with lockjaw.'

'Hardly, in this day and age. I must say I rather like the thought of going to Putney. A 30 bus goes all the way and there are trains. Yes, I think I'll risk the lockjaw. Are you going now, dear? You look a little peaky; an early night will do you good.'

Ivy had hardly left the room before Berti heard Evelyn's key turning in the front-door. She darted out and, clutching her arm, hissed, 'Quick, come into the drawing-room for a minute. I've some news for you about Ivy's lover: I think I know who he is. My God, it's the funniest thing that has ever happened. He's a Putney dentist and I'm making an appointment with him tomorrow.'

On Monday morning Amy took her coat from the hall stand and prepared to accompany Hetty to school; but the girl returned the coat to its hook and said, 'There really is no need for you to come with me, Mummy. It's too cold to play truant now. Anyway, I don't want to lose my part as the Madonna. We are rehearsing like mad now.'

Amy studied her daughter thoughtfully. 'Well, dear, if you are sure I can trust you, it would be such a help not to spend all that time travelling. It's my day for the launderette, too. By the way, I never asked you. What were you and young Solly doing on Sunday afternoon? You were away for over an hour.'

Hetty laughed. 'Really, Mummy. We only went down to the river to see if the tide was out. You can get right down on the beach when it is; heavenly, all swans, mud and buried treasure.'

Amy helped her on with her coat. 'You know I don't like you traipsing about with that ugly boy.'

'Poor Solly, he can't help looking like Caliban.'

'Caliban! Wasn't he a character in I.T.M.A.? Fancy you knowing that. Such a lovely programme it was.' Amy followed her daughter to the gate, hoping she was doing the right thing. In spite of the grey day she felt almost cheerful. Hetty seemed to be growing up at last, and her troublesome tenants had been quieter the last few weeks, not so many rings on the bell or noisy nights. Only that morning she had heard Berti telephoning the dentist that Doris had recommended, quite sensibly, like any other elderly lady. Usually if anything went wrong with her, she would wrap herself up in an almost-bald fur coat and swear and moan until she recovered. Once or twice Amy had been so alarmed, she had called in her own doctor and paid the bill herself. Neither Berti nor Evelyn paid any contribution to National Insurance, so were barred from free medical attention and pensions. 'What's going to happen to them when they are really old, I can't imagine. They can't see as far as their noses,' she often remarked to Doris, who would shrug her shoulders and say, 'They're not your pigeon. They'll be looked after, people like that always are.' It was easy for Doris, who didn't have them living in the house.

Amy examined the rose-bushes in the front garden and sighed over the suckers which were draining their vitality. What would Alf have thought to see his roses so neglected. 'I suppose I could cut them off with the carving knife,' she thought ruefully as she went down to the basement to collect her bundle of soiled sheets for the laundrette. 'I'll never get used to Alf dying like that.'

There was a state of excitement going on upstairs because, after several disappointments, Berti had managed to contact 'Cocky' on the telephone and after a rather abrupt conversation it had been arranged that he would take her out to luncheon.

'I do want you all to meet him,' Berti screeched with nervous excitement, her toothache all forgotten. 'Evelyn, you'll be here, won't you? I'll run up to the Señora and ask her to come down. Cocky will be fascinated by her. Be an angel, Evelyn, and buy another bottle of whisky. He drinks it neat by the tumblerful. I do want to make a good impression; he could make a tremendous difference to our lives, bring all his friends here and that sort of thing. Put new life into our little business.' She rushed up to the Señora's room at the top of the house and burst in without knocking.

The Señora, who was arranging her beautiful black-dyed hair, looked startled and, ignoring Berti, continued with her hair. One white lock was allowed to flow through the darkness to add to the dramatic effect and it needed careful arrangement. When she was satisfied with her appearance she turned to Berti who was shaking with excitement. Yes, the Señora would be glad to meet Mr Cocky for a few minutes before her appointment with her manicurist. How many years was it since Mrs Berti had seen the gentleman? she wanted to know.

Berti, casting her mind back, realized it must be at least twenty-five, not ten as she had thought. 'But even if he has aged a bit, he'll still be Cocky and frightfully amusing,' she said happily. 'Drinks like a fish, yet I've never seen him drunk, really drunk. Do you think I should wear the red pants or the new black velvet? I suppose it depends on where he's taking me for luncheon. Oh, Lord, if it's the Ritz I'll have to wear a skirt.' She ran down to her room to change into the black velvet pants.

At a quarter-to-one the three women were waiting for Cocky in the drawing-room. Ivy was selling her skeins of wool in Gloucester Road and missing the great event.

Berti already had a drink in her hand. 'I must have something to steady myself. I'm shaking with nerves. You don't think this blue eye-shadow is too much, do you, Evelyn?'

Evelyn shook her head although she thought Berti was looking a mess. 'What do you think, Señora?'

The Señora studied her between narrowed eyes and suggested that they went to Berti's room for a moment while she 'smoothed it in a little'.

As they were leaving the room, the bell rang. 'My God! Here he is!' Berti cried as she scuttled towards the front door. A minute or two later she returned with Henn-Crosby, otherwise Cocky. He was a heavily built man wearing a dark suit and carrying a particularly hard-looking bowler hat. His grey hair was cut short and, except for his glassy, slightly bloodshot eyes, he had the air of a family lawyer.

Berti introduced him and he gravely bowed and, looking round the florid room, remarked, 'What a strange drawing-room you have, Berti; I have been somewhere rather like this before.'

She giggled. 'Oh, it isn't really mine, we share it. Now, what about a drink? I'm sure you're dying for one.'

He held up a forbidding hand. 'No, not for me. Never

touch the stuff; poison, absolute poison.' He glanced at his watch. 'I don't want to hurry you, Berti, but if you are lunching with me we had better leave. It won't take long to change, will it?' Berti gave an agonized look at her velvet slacks, gulped down her whisky and left the room, with her shoulders hunched up to her ears.

'Well, well, you seem to have found a pleasant little backwater here,' Cocky said as he stood by the window tapping his arm with his folded gloves.

'Yes,' the Señora agreed, 'it is very pleasant. I have lived here for over eight years now.'

Evelyn chirped in, 'And Berti and I for six, we both answered the same advertisement.'

'Did you indeed?' he said in a bored voice. 'Ah, I think I hear Berti!' He picked up his bowler hat, stiffly bowed and strode into the hall. 'Sorry to rush you, Berti, but I have an appointment at three. My car is just round the corner,' they heard. The front door closed and the oddly assorted couple walked towards the gate.

'Good grief, she's wearing my suede coat,' Evelyn exclaimed, and would have made a dash to tear it off Berti's back if the Señora had not restrained her.

'Let her be, poor woman. I see she is also wearing my new gloves.'

Evelyn was alone when Berti returned. She rushed into the room, gasping, 'Yes, I know I borrowed your coat, thank you very much. Wait until I tell you what I've been through. I've had the most fearful time, I can't believe a man could change so much in a few years. My dear, guess where he took me — to a vegetarian restaurant; nothing but grated carrot and nuts, a few lettuce leaves and a disgusting concoction which might have been semolina flavoured with cheese. Nothing to drink except fruit juice, all healthy and horrible. He calls meat-eaters "blood addicts". He's turned into a health fiend and goes to those fearfully expensive hydros where they give you enemas all the time. I think he must have had a slight stroke or cirrhosis of the liver or something, anyway, he is always having check-ups. Doesn't smoke either. When I had a cigarette with coffee, he kept holding his handkerchief to his nose. I'd been so looking forward to telling him about our professional life, but of course I couldn't now he's become such a prig. We did talk a little about old times and once or twice he almost laughed, but all he is really interested in is self and health with a capital H. It *was* a disappointment. Now all I have to look forward to is Ivy's dentist. By the way, is the Señora out? I want to return these gloves to her room.'

Evelyn smiled. 'I think she's upstairs; she noticed you were wearing them.' She enjoyed Berti's discomfort. They were all a little afraid of the dark-eyed Catalan.

Berti examined the gloves dubiously. 'I don't seem to have done them much harm. I only wore one and carried the other. I suppose I'd better go up and face her and return your coat at the same time. You can borrow my new mohair stole if you like.' Evelyn nodded; she had intended to borrow the stole in any case. She got up and went towards the window to draw the heavy crimson curtains and stood for a moment looking out at the dusky winter afternoon. A policeman was coming round a corner of the square and, when he reached Amy's gate, hesitated a moment, then opened it and walked into the neglected garden. She was relieved to see him going down to the basement.

Amy opened the door and there he was, playing his cat and mouse game. She stood without speaking, no incriminating statements were going to pass her lips if she could help it.

The policeman looked at the closed little face and smiled. 'Sorry to disturb you again, but you mentioned that you were on your own and I wondered if you'd like any help in the garden. It happens that I've been given a few bulbs and rose-bushes and, having no garden myself, I was wondering what to do with them. It's my free day tomorrow and it'd be a kindness if you'd let me put in a few hours here.'

Amy gave him a quick look, then lowered her lids while she considered his proposition. 'If he wants to spy on us,' she thought, 'nothing will stop him, so he may as well make himself useful while he's about it. I could get him to take down those rusty bells for a start and the lino in the scullery wants re-laying.' She smiled.

'Well, if you're sure you want to spend your free time gardening, I'd be grateful; there's quite a bit at the back, you know.'

'Yes, I thought there might be. Could I have a glance at it for a moment?' Amy led him through the basement passage and opened the garden door and they walked into the almost-dark garden together. 'What do you use all those tall sticks for? Tomatoes?' He peered at the dead, headless stalks of the sunflowers.

Amy laughed. 'They are only the remains of the sunflowers I grow for an old gentleman's parrot,' she said, then put her hand to her mouth – 'Incriminating evidence, I shouldn't have mentioned old Mr Gore,' she thought as she peered at the policeman in the dusk, but he didn't appear to have noticed; he was tugging at a sunflower stalk and saying something about 'greedy feeders'.

He wandered round the garden with the mop-ended

stalk in his hand. 'I'm glad it's been neglected; I'm longing to get my hands on it,' he said enthusiastically as they returned to the house. 'By the way, have you any gardening tools? I could borrow them otherwise.' Amy remembered the shed under the steps where Alf had kept his tools; she supposed they were still there.

She said, 'I think I have all you will need, only they'll be a bit rusty. I'll unlock the shed in the morning and see what's there. What time shall I expect you, then?' she asked as she hurried him out of the house. He must be gone before Hetty returned. At least he wouldn't be wearing his uniform tomorrow. When he had gone, she realized she didn't know his name. She must ask him immediately he arrived. It didn't seem nice having a man about the garden and not knowing what he was called.

When he came the next day he told her his name was Harry Lake and he lived with his married brother and his wife Fulham way. He said he had been engaged to a girl who had died of polio some years ago. 'Fair she was and a lovely dancer. Terrible, her dying like that. Only ill for three days, just a bit of a throat to begin with. On the Saturday she said, 'Oh, Harry, I don't think I'll go dancing tonight. My throat feels so fearful.' She was all dressed up and ready, too, and that was the last time I saw her, standing in her mother's hall in her blue dress. She was taken to hospital on the Monday and died the following day. I've never got over the shock of her dying like that and I've never been dancing again.

They sat drinking coffee in the basement room and Amy had almost forgotten that he was there to spy. She told him about Alf's death from an operation that had gone wrong, for all he was so healthy, and about Hetty being educated above her station although it was a struggle to pay the fees. 'Alf was set on it, you see, and I don't want to let him down.' She kept off the subject of her tenants. She hoped they wouldn't come nosing round the garden while he was working there. Perhaps it would be better to warn them.

They went to the shed and inspected the tools and Harry Lake said the damp earth would clear most of the rust away and he'd oil them after use. His idea was to dig over the entire garden and redesign it. The dusty privet was condemned and the long, straggling vine was to be cut back. He hoped he would be able to save the roses, although they had been weakened by suckers, and he'd plant a lawn in the spring unless she preferred crazy paving. He talked with great enthusiasm and it seemed as if he planned to spend a considerable time in the garden. 'If I get sent to prison, I suppose he'll come here just the same,' she thought as she left him digging the damp clay and went to speak to her ladies. It was really only Berti and Evelyn who needed warning, the other two were discreet.

She found Evelyn in Berti's room trying on her mauve stole.

'It looks far better on me,' she said as she turned before the looking-glass. 'It doesn't go with Berti's dyed-red hair. It's a wonder she's got any left. The things she does with it. One day she'll lose the lot and won't even be eligible for a National Health wig. Mine's naturally curly and feel how thick and strong it is, Mrs Doll, just feel it.'

Amy agreed that she had a fine head of hair. 'But what I've really come about is to tell you that there's a policeman in the garden. If you look through the back windows you'll see him there, bent over his spade.'

Evelyn turned away from her reflection. 'Heavens! Is he looking for a body?' she asked eagerly. 'The murderer, Haigh, lived somewhere round here, didn't he?'

Amy gave a downward smile. 'No, it isn't a body he's looking for. He's just keeping an eye on the place and doing a bit of gardening at the same time, so we'd better mind our p's and q's while he's around. Perhaps you'd mention it to Miss Berti.'

Alone again, Evelyn smeared Berti's blue eye-shadow on her lids, then went to the bathroom window to gaze down on the policeman. He was a good-looking man of about thirty-five, his hair very glossy and dark, and Evelyn thought, if only the men who came to her were young and firm and with hair it was a pleasure to touch. 'Oh, God,' she thought, 'I'm so sick of these worn-out old men who are never satisfied. I loathe them and Harry Rutter most of all. Mean dwarf! He always stands with his silly head thrown back as if he were about to gargle. What a mess I've made of my life; if only I had a home of my own and some security. My only sister hasn't spoken to me for years, I can't remember why. Perhaps there's something wrong with me, my marriage only lasting a year and I haven't a real friend in the world, forcing myself on people with my bottle of cheap wine and those wretched Sundays at Twickenham, when no one listens to a word I say and the children turn their backs on me and play their horrible records. Hetty may be fond of me in her vague way. I must make an effort and do more for the child. Oh, well, Berti will be back soon and I'll hear about this dentist.' Evelyn ended her soliloquy with a vague little wave to the policeman and, shutting the window, went down to have her first drink of the day.

A little later, Berti staggered into the drawing-room,

wailing. 'That man! Doris said he was a smasher and he certainly is. The bloody fool's smashed my jaw. Pulled out a tooth and filled another with only a local anaesthetic. My mouth feels so stange I can hardly speak. Pour me out a glass of brandy, I feel about to faint.' She sank onto the sofa, rocking backwards and forwards and holding her jaw as if it was in danger of falling off. Evelyn impatiently pushed a glass of neat brandy into her hand and waited for the news. Was the dentist Ivy's lover or wasn't he? She knew from past experience that it was no good rushing Berti.

'My lips are all dead; I can't feel the glass,' she wailed. 'He gave me some tablets to take; be a dear and get them out of my bag.' Evelyn rummaged about in the worn crocodile handbag, Berti's most treasured possession, and produced the tablets. Berti took one and let it slowly dissolve on her tongue, then washed it down with neat brandy, gasping and pulling faces as she did so.

Evelyn, who could bear it no longer, said, 'I'm going to the kitchen to do something about lunch. Can't make up my mind what to have, baked beans or soup or perhaps sardines.' Amy had turned a cloakroom into a tiny kitchen for her tenants; but the Señora was the only one who made real use of it, the others lived on food from packets or tins.

Evelyn walked slowly towards the door and Berti, putting down her glass, cried, 'You're not going, are you? Don't you want to hear my news?'

Evelyn glanced over her shoulder. 'Tell me when you're feeling a little better, dear.'

Berti sprang from the sofa. 'I am feeling better, I've practically recovered except for this bloody silly lip.'

Evelyn turned away from the door and folded her

long arms. 'All right, fire away, then I'll warm you up some soup. Of course, I'm dying to know what happened,' she added encouragingly.

Berti took another sip of brandy, holding it on the sore side of her mouth for a moment to deaden the pain. 'I was right. This dentist, he's called Thomson, Hugh Thomson, is Ivy's lover. As soon as I gave him my address he looked surprised, then told me he'd been to the house, a friend of his lived there. I asked if he meant Ivy and he said he did and wanted to know if she'd sent me. I told him the truth, that Ivy was all against it and it was Doris Moon who'd sent me. I wished I hadn't said that afterwards because he changed the subject and before I could bring it back to Ivy he had me sitting in that revolving chair with my mouth wide open. Every time I tried to speak, he rammed something in my mouth. At one time it was packed with cotton wool. I felt too ill to say much by the time he'd finished. I did ask if he had a message for Ivy, but he pretended he didn't hear and I was rushed out by one of those idiot girls dressed like nurses.'

Evelyn helped herself to one of Berti's cigarettes. 'What sort of a man is he?' she asked.

'Rather insignificant, not bad-looking though; about forty-five, I should say. The annoying thing is that I don't think I would recognize him again if I saw him in the street. He's that kind of man, a typical Thomson. I really didn't learn much, definitely not worth all this pain, and I suppose he'll send a bill. Why don't you go and have a session with him? I'm sure your teeth need some attention. It's years since you went.'

Evelyn made for the kitchen. She knew Berti's next remark would refer to her protruding teeth. She shouted from the kitchen, 'Well, what kind of soup do you want? There's chicken or tomato in tins and a packet of mushroom. Make your choice.'

'It doesn't matter; whichever you're having,' Berti said bleakly.

That evening, as Hugh Thomson and Ivy sat hand in hand before his glowing gas fire, he said, 'A funny thing happened this morning. A very tall old woman wearing scarlet trousers turned up and said she lives in the same house as you. Jago, I think she was called. Her mouth was in a shocking state, continental crowning on bad roots.'

Ivy stiffened. 'Well, what did she say about me?'

The dentist laughed. 'She said something about you not recommending her, but she couldn't say much with her mouth wide open. She seemed a bit inquisitive, though. Poor old thing, she must have been quite something when she was young.'

5

Ivy was in the basement having a heart-to-heart talk with Amy. Heart-to-heart talks with her tenants had become a sort of occupational hazard for Amy and wasted hours of her time.

Ivy, curled up in the only comfortable chair, said, 'If Hugh knew the sort of life I was leading here, it would be the end of everything. As it is, there is quite a chance of him marrying me. We get on so well together and I'm only four years older than he is. You don't think that matters, do you, Mrs Doll?'

Amy glanced up from the knitting pattern she was puzzling over. 'No, of course not. I wish I'd never started this complicated thing.'

Ivy went on, 'What do you advise me to do, Mrs Doll? Should I leave the house and get away from them? I never wanted to get mixed up in their horrible plans, but, only earning eight pounds a week, what could I do? They make far more than I do out of it. The Señora, for instance, must earn pounds and even on a good week I only make about two pounds fifteen, and that widower, he expects so much for his money and completely exhausts me.'

Amy frowned. 'K.7,k.2. tog, t.b.1., k.16. Yes, I believe the Señora has done quite well for herself. She has been saving money for years and is hoping to start a little hotel – *pension* she calls it – in her own country. She'll be leaving quite soon. Now. K.2. tog., t.b.1., k. to end.'

For a moment Ivy forgot her troubles. 'Do you mean the Señora's leaving, after all these years? Why, she was here when your husband was alive; you must have been quite a girl when she first came.'

Amy smiled. 'Well, not exactly a girl. I must have been twenty-seven when she first came to live with us, but staid, I've always been that way inclined. She put down her knitting. 'Drat the thing. It's a pig I'm knitting for a kiddy and shaping the mouth is so difficult.'

Ivy glanced at the pink and grey mess of wool. 'I can hardly bear to look at it,' she said. 'These women, buying ounces of wool all day long, quite an unhealthy craving, I sometimes think. I like selling the silks and the customers sometimes show me the pretty things they have embroidered. I'd rather like to take it up myself. I could start with table mats and if I married – Oh, Mrs Doll, would it be any good if you spoke to Berti and Evelyn and asked them not to interfere between Hugh and me? Berti would have ruined everything if Hugh hadn't stopped up her mouth with cotton wool. All the dentists in London and she had to pick on him.'

Amy got up to put the kettle on. Hetty would be home from school soon. 'I shouldn't worry, Miss Ivy,' she said as she hunted for the matches. 'Miss Berti doesn't like pain. I don't think she'll go there again.' She bustled about with a string of sausages and a frying pan and Ivy reluctantly left her chair. At least she had something to tell them upstairs. She was sure they hadn't heard the Señora's plans. She knew they would both want her large room when she left; it was the best bedroom in the house. Their quarrelling would take their minds off her affairs. She tripped upstairs. It was her evening for the impoverished chiropodist.

On Mondays and Thursdays Harry Lake came to dig the garden. Although it was late in the year, rose trees had been planted and a lilac bush, which would in time bear deep purple sprays, he said. He also planted a bed of tulips mixed with Spanish iris and, when Amy offered to pay for the bulbs, he told her they had come from a friend's garden, although she had seen him furtively stuffing a box marked with the name of Sutton into the dustbin. She thought that perhaps the bulbs had been provided by the police to give Harry Lake an excuse to spy on the house.

Once he had come in from the garden saying, 'Your tenants look a rum lot. I saw two of them hanging out of one of the windows this morning, a red-head and a blue. How many of them are there?'

Amy stammered, 'How many? I don't know, four I think. Yes, of course, there are four of them. All of good family, one is a bishop's daughter, so she says. They are widows and that sort of thing, but on the eccentric side.' She hurried to the scullery to make coffee. 'I hope the garden gets finished before they pounce on me,' she thought. 'If I'm only fined with a caution it'll be almost worth it, except for the disgrace. It would be bound to get into *The Kensington Post*.'

Harry Rutter was holding forth to Berti and Evelyn.

'What you need here is a piano. When I lived in Madrid I always used to go to one of the brothels when I felt the need to play the piano. The girls used to love it.' He threw back his head and sang a few notes. 'Did Evelyn tell you, Berti, about the delightful little place I took her to on Sunday? I get special service at all these places and it makes such a difference. Where is little Ivy this evening?'

Berti sneered. 'The silly little fool is keeping to her room. She's all dreamy-eyed about a dentist and I upset her by visiting him professionally. Thinks I'm going to steal him, I suppose.'

Evelyn put down her glass and drawled, 'She told me there are going to be changes in the house; when I asked her what changes, she did a great mystery act. You don't think sweet little Amy is going to turf us all out, do you?'

Harry Rutter gave his thin little laugh. 'Of course not. She knows which side her bread is buttered. Even if she did, with my influence I'd find you somewhere just as good in a matter of days.'

Berti snapped, 'If you've got so much influence, why don't you find somewhere better to live yourself. It must be hell in that scruffy little hotel.'

'My dear Berti, I adore my scruffy little hotel. It's simply crammed with atmosphere. Reminds me of Paris before the war and the women who run it are sweeties. They'd do anything for me.'

Berti gave him a withering look and left the room. As she closed the door she heard Evelyn say, 'You see what I mean, she's always so unnecessarily rude.'

Berti made her way to Ivy's small room at the top of the house. She knocked at the door and Ivy peered through a chink expecting to see Hetty or her mother. Her face fell when she saw the formidable Berti.

'Can I come in, Ivy?' she asked sweetly and was in the room before Ivy could summon enough courage to shut the door in her face. 'What a nice room this is and you have made it so cosy. I haven't been up here for years.' Her eyes darted round, taking in the pink candlewick cover on the bed, the pillows disguised as cushions, the photograph of the late Mr Rope and the late Mr and Mrs Gray, Ivy's parents, and lastly the set of table mats Ivy was embroidering with flowers. She hastily pushed them into a drawer and stood in front as if she were defending state documents.

Berti said, 'Do you mind if I sit down, dear?' and perched on the only chair, a hard little thing with wooden arms. She looked calculatingly at Ivy still pressed against the chest of drawers. 'Darling,' she cooed, 'I'm afraid I've upset you, but I'd no idea that that nice dentist was anything to do with you until you behaved so peculiarly over that piece of paper Doris had given me. She said he was perfectly marvellous, so of course I went to him; but I promise I won't visit him again, even if I'm in agony with toothache. He really is the most charming man, no wonder you want to keep him to yourself. I don't want to be nosy. Is there any chance of him marrying you?'

'I've no idea,' Ivy replied coldly. 'He certainly won't if you and Evelyn go out of your way to wreck things.'

Berti fished in her pocket for cigarettes, offered one to Ivy, who shook her head. 'Sorry, of course, you don't smoke. I always forget.' She lit her cigarette and gazed pensively through the smoke, then said, 'I swear I won't do a thing to mess your chance of marrying and I'm sure Evelyn won't either when I've spoken to her. You mentioned a divorce. Is it through yet?'

'Yes, it was made absolute nearly a month ago and I hoped he'd say something, but he hasn't.' Lowering her voice, she added, 'I'd be the happiest woman in the world if he did ask me to marry him.'

Berti found her former spite and jealousy melting away as she said gruffly, 'He'll be a damn fool if he doesn't. You'd make a splended little wife and be such a help with the patients.'

After that, Ivy opened the drawer and showed Berti the table mats she was embroidering and an elderly photograph of her family home at Wimbledon. 'Not grand like the ones you and Evelyn lived in, but so comfortable. There was a tennis court at the back – you can just see the big pear tree on the right – and we had a swing. My sister and I went to the Wimbledon High School. I'm afraid I was a bit of a dunce, though. My parents gave us such a happy home and were so good to us. I'd have loved to have had a child myself, but my husband, Mr Rope, was against it.'

Over cups of Nescafé she told Berti that the Señora was leaving in the spring. Berti had forgotten the real reason that had caused her to visit Ivy's room; now she begged her not to mention to Evelyn that the Señora was leaving. 'I must ask Amy if I can have her room, it's the best in the house,' she said excitedly, 'with all those cupboards and two windows. I'll talk to Amy about it tomorrow.' The telephone began to ring and she darted away to answer it. They parted the best of friends.

The following Sunday, when Ivy went to Putney, her dentist lover told her that his receptionist was leaving to emigrate with her parents. 'As soon as I train them something like this happens,' he said irritably. Laying a hand on Ivy's shoulder, he looked at her thoughtfully. 'It's an extraordinary coincidence, really. I don't think

I've mentioned to you that I'm thinking of emigrating to Canada myself. Forty-seven is rather old to take such a step, but my sister, Frances, and her husband live in Toronto and keep urging me to join them; they say there are wonderful prospects for dentists and I've practically made up my mind to go. What do you think about it, Mouse?'

'I think it would be the saddest thing that has ever happened to me,' she said, putting her hand over his. 'Please don't go.'

The dentist looked at her quivering face with amazement. 'But why do you dislike the idea of Canada so much?' he asked. 'Surely you don't think I'd leave you behind?'

'But do you mean I can come too?' she asked, her eyes swimming with tears.

He drew her to him. 'Of course I do, you silly Mouse. I thought it was taken for granted that we'd marry when the divorce came through. I didn't mention it before because of this Canadian idea. I wanted to make a few enquiries first and there'll be the practice to dispose of. If we go it's going to make the hell of an upheaval but I think it will be worth it. What do you think, my dear? Shall we go?'

'Yes, yes, let's go,' Ivy cried enthusiastically. 'I'd so love to start again with you — a completely new life. How long must we wait?' To be released from Mulberry Grove, Berti, Evelyn and the chiropodist and, above all, from the widower who came on Wednesdays. Never to see them again. No more women clamouring for knitting-wool, no more listening to the manageress talking about her home knitting machine and her fallen arches. She would be thousands of miles away, married to her wonderful Hugh and her disagreeable past behind her.

On the Wednesday evening, the night of the widower, Ivy rushed home from the shop and burst into the drawing-room, exclaiming with a note of hysteria in her voice, 'I won't be here when he comes. I never want to see him again. If either of you want him, you are welcome, but I warn you, he pinches.' Slamming the door, she ran from the house as if it were about to explode.

'What do you make of that?' Evelyn asked.

The Señora looked up from her sewing and said, 'I think it means she's taken a dislike to the *viudo*.'

Berti smiled. 'I think it means wedding bells are in the offing, and a damn good thing too.'

Evelyn said, 'She's certainly worked for it. She didn't have much success with the *viudo*, did she?'

'Just as well; this man is a far better proposition. I don't think I'll take on the pincher. Do you want him, Evelyn?'

'I might, if he wants me.' She laughed. 'It's almost Christmas and I haven't saved a penny. Do you remember last year when they all went off to their families and no one came near us for days?'

The Señora folded her sewing and remarked, 'I will be in Spain for Christmas and will stay until after the Three Kings.' And sailed from the room.

'What a lot of shocks we are having this evening!' Berti said with a hiccup, and both of them laughed.

A day or two later, when Harry Lake was working in the garden, Amy came out and said, 'One of my ladies is leaving to get married.'

'What! One of those crazy old girls upstairs?'

'This one isn't really old. She works in a haberdasher's near the tube station. She's a widow, poor thing.

Very respectable, her father was a solicitor from Wimbledon.'

Harry Lake bent to pull up a weed. 'They come up quick, don't they? The ground elder I've dug up in this garden! What will you do with the room, then? Let it again?'

'I really don't know,' she replied as she pulled up a sprig of groundsel. 'That's what's bothering me. A new lady mightn't get on with the others. To tell the truth, I'd like to get shot of the lot and start again, perhaps with gentlemen. Not old ones, gentlemen who go out to work and stay out all day.' She examined the groundsel closely. 'It's quite a pretty little flower really. Canaries like it. Yes, all things considered, I think gentlemen would be better.'

Harry frowned. 'You'd never manage a lot of men. You'd be running after them all day, making their beds and seeing to their laundry, and they'd take it all for granted. You stick to your ladies; but choose better next time.'

Choose better. What did he mean by that? Not choose a lot of old tarts, I suppose, Amy thought as she left the policeman to his gardening. It was her day for Hoovering the house and every now and then she'd switch off the machine and have a look out of the back windows. It was nice to have a man about the place and, although it was winter, the garden looked so hopeful, almost spring-like. It was a pity there was so little left to do now, but the neglected patch in the front still remained. Perhaps Harry would take that on too. Her ladies had been behaving very quietly lately, it was as if they sensed danger; and now she was losing two. She sighed. She was still saddled with the two that caused her the most anxiety and now Berti was pestering her for the Señora's room. She returned to the Hoovering.

6

The marriage of Ivy and Hugh was arranged to take place the Saturday before Christmas. It was to be a quiet ceremony with Amy Doll and a dentist friend of Hugh's as witnesses. Afterwards, they planned to drink champagne in a nearby hotel and then drive off for a few days' honeymoon at Eastbourne.

'It's all so respectable and ordinary, except for the registry office. I do wish we could have been married in a church,' Ivy confided to Amy when she asked her to act as witness. 'You don't think those two upstairs will come and spoil everything, do you, Mrs Doll? I could bring home a bottle of champagne on my last evening here and have a little celebration. I've told them the wedding is to take place at twelve instead of eleven, but they are quite capable of going round to the office and making their own enquiries. I shan't feel safe until I'm on the boat, with England well behind me.'

On the floor above, Evelyn and Berti were discussing the same subject: the Rope-Thomson wedding.

'You don't think she's going to invite us, then?' Evelyn asked as she studied her reflection in one of the gilt mirrors. She decided it was time she visited her hairdresser; the blue was fading.

'Well, she hasn't said anything about us being present at the ceremony or anything, and there's less than a week to go. Poor little bitch, I can't blame her. What about having a party for her on the last night? We could ask all the old boys and give her a real send-off. I'm sure they would help with the drinks. We could make it a sort of Christmas party and have a decorated tree.'

'I don't think they'd enjoy a kid's party with a tree; you'll be suggesting jellies next,' Evelyn said contemptuously.

'We could decorate the tree with contraceptives – and what are those things, purple hearts?'

'What foul ideas you have! How about hiring a record-player and buying a few records and we could have copies of *Playboy* lying about and a few nudes pinned on the walls – photographs, not real ones.'

'If they want nudes, they've got me,' Berti snapped. 'I'll do one of my dances and you could wear a topless dress. You are always going on about your bust, I can't think why. It's fallen.'

'What was that you said? Thank heaven, I'm not flat-chested. A woman without a bust isn't a real woman,' Evelyn sneered, then, gazing at her reflection again, adjusted the straps of her brassière. 'To make the party really go, we need a few pretty girls – dollies, dolly-girls, chicks or whatever they're called at the moment. When all's said and done, we're not as young as we were.'

'Dolly-girls! How vulgar can you get?' Berti screamed. 'I wouldn't have let one cross the threshold – a lot of bloody beatniks and drug addicts.' Then, thoughtfully, 'I suppose Amy wouldn't come? She's not bad-looking when she's dressed properly.'

'Impossible. Far too strait-laced and she has parlour-maid written all over her. It's a pity Hetty is so young, but her mother would never let her come and I wouldn't like to contaminate the child. Let her keep her innocence for a few more years.'

Berti flicked her cigarette on the carpet. 'I wouldn't say she was all that innocent. What do you imagine she does when she plays truant all day? Of course, she is messing about with boys or men or both. It wouldn't surprise me if she turned into one of those teenage mothers. She's losing her looks anyway; far too tall for her age and all that hair hanging down. I'll tell Amy to have it cut off.'

'Well, I'll tell her to keep it on. All the girls are wearing their hair like that and I think it's most attractive. You're jealous because the child's growing up.'

'Growing up! She's so retarded even her mother is worried about it, says she's always been inclined that way. She is sly, too, those kind of children always are. My God, what's that?'

They hurried to the window and saw a great pile of broken paving stones had been dumped outside the house.

'That's a damn silly thing to do,' Berti cried through the glass to a retreating van. 'How do you think we are going to get out? Do you think we are bloody chamois?'

'Do you think they come from tombs?' Evelyn asked anxiously.

'No, they are the kind you walk on; paving.'

Amy emerged from the basement and stood staring at her blocked gateway. Then Harry Lake appeared and, laughing, climbed over the stones and proceeded to stack them neatly in the front garden. Amy worked with him and the watching women noticed that he only allowed her to lift the smaller stones.

'He's considerate, that man, no one ever considers us,' Evelyn said in a moment of truth. She longed to help in the heaving of stones, but Amy had given her a look and shaken her head in a forbidding manner.

Hetty returned from school and joined the figures working in the dusk. 'Not in that coat,' her mother said sharply and she ran into the house and returned wearing an outgrown crimson one with a torn pocket.

It was dark when they finished and, as Evelyn drew the curtains, she said, 'My cousins at Twickenham have miles of crazy paving, two long paths and a terrace.'

'Gnomes and toadstools, too, I expect.' Berti poured herself the first drink of the evening, an unusually small one. She was expecting a new client that evening, a middle-aged Greek she had met in the underground. He had just buried his wife, he said, and was feeling lonely. She felt nervous; he was so dark and his melancholy eyes were like dates. He told her his wife had died in the street. A street accident? Murdered? He did not say.

Harry Lake stayed for high-tea; bubble and squeak with an egg on top and tinned pineapple. He asked Hetty if she would like to be a policewoman when she grew up, but she said she'd rather be married. When he had gone, she asked her mother who he was. It was the first time she had met him. Amy told her he was the gardener. Hetty thought for a moment, then said, 'Oh, he seems more like a friend.'

Amy flushed. 'Yes, I suppose he has turned into a friend, but I mustn't forget he's a policeman and has his duty to do.'

* * *

Ivy said goodbye to the manageress with the fallen arches and left the haberdashery shop for the last time. She was to be married the following morning. On the way home she stopped at an off-licence and bought a bottle of champagne for Berti and Evelyn. The Señora had already left for her Spanish holiday. 'I'll just have a sip with them, then go up to my room. Please, God, don't let them have bought presents for me so that I'll feel guilty about not asking them to the wedding.'

As soon as she opened the front door the house felt different. There were flowers on the hall table, great yellow chrysanthemums, and a man's hat perched on the bannisters. Clutching the champagne, she slowly opened the drawing-room door. She nearly dropped the bottle. The room was all prepared for a party, more flowers, plates of food, glasses and bottles, an electric gramophone and a sad-looking Greek reading *Playboy*.

Evelyn rushed into the room, wearing skin-tight green tights and a black and gold tunic, her hair a startling blue-mauve. 'Ivy,' she shrieked excitedly, 'hurry upstairs and change. We are giving a surprise party for you. Everyone's coming, we've been working on it all day. Don't look so worried, we haven't asked the pinching widower.'

Berti skimmed in, kissing the Greek on both cheeks, and spun round like a top in front of Ivy and Evelyn. She appeared to have a pair of dehydrated moths on her eyes. 'Do you like them, dears? False eyelashes. I found them at the back of one of the drawers, must be at least ten years old, but very alluring.' She fluttered the dehydrated moths over her almost-closed eyes.

'Can you see with them?' Ivy asked bleakly.

'Not very well, but as long as I can see my drink, that's all that matters. I say, is that champagne? Put it on the table with the other bottles before you drop it, dear.'

Evelyn was still staring at the eyelashes. 'How have you fixed them?' she enquired.

'Actually, with glue. There wasn't anything else. It stings a bit. Do you think they look all right?'

'Frankly, no. I'm not being bitchy, but they look a mess. Get them off before they set too hard.'

Berti walked to one of the mirrors and, lifting her eyelashes with her little fingers, gazed at her reflection. 'Perhaps you're right,' she said resignedly, then snapped, 'those your new pants? Far too tight and the colour of chewed grass. What ever made you choose them?'

The Greek went on turning the pages of *Playboy*, completely oblivious to what was going on in the room.

Ivy stood irresolutely, trying to pluck up courage to say she was tired and not up to a party. 'If you don't mind,' she faltered, 'I'd prefer to have a drink of champagne with you both, then go up to bed. I haven't finished my packing yet and really don't feel up to a party.'

'What the hell do you mean?' Berti demanded, tugging at her false eyelashes. 'The party's for you. We have been slaving away at it all day, besides spending a fortune on drink. Of course you must be here. Oh, God, there's someone at the door and I haven't got these things off yet. Run upstairs and put on something suitable. You'll feel quite different when you've had a drink. Bride's nerves, that's what is wrong with you.'

She danced off to open the door to Jim Clarke and Evelyn, taking Ivy firmly by the arm, said, 'I'll help you dress,' and marched her up to her room.

The little room was filled with closed cases and a trunk, and the only thing left in the wardrobe was the wedding dress, gleaming blue from under a plastic cover, like a flower in a greenhouse. Evelyn pounced on it and Ivy, snatching it from her, hung it back in the wardrobe and produced a black cocktail dress of uncertain age.

Evelyn eyed it doubtfully. 'Black for a bride! You can't wear black. What about this green one?' and she pulled it out of the trunk, scattering tissue paper as she did so.

Ivy sighed, took off her brown working dress and threw it into the waste-paper basket. 'I never want to see that again. Perhaps Amy Doll can make some use of it. Oh dear, I did so want an early night.' She slowly dressed and made up her face, Evelyn tweaking and touching her like a nervous fly.

They went downstairs together, Ivy trailing behind Evelyn, who ran down the last flight to embrace Harry Rutter, who had just arrived and was standing with his head thrown back and his chin jutting forward. He disentangled himself from Evelyn and, advancing on Ivy, moistly kissed her on the lips. From the hall table he lifted a bottle wrapped in gaudy Christmas paper and, handing it to Evelyn with a flourish, said, 'You asked me to bring a bottle, ducky, and here it is. Beer; so refreshing, I thought, for later in the evening.' Evelyn icily told him to put it with the other drinks in the drawing-room.

The party started badly. The Greek continued to read *Playboy* and Harry Rutter, between sandwiches, held forth about his visits to Madame Patti's house in Barcelona, when he worked as an accountant there a good ten years ago, and Jim Clarke quavered about his visits to Paris houses a good thirty years ago. Evelyn played the gramophone, but no one listened. Berti sat beside the Greek, giving him a highly-coloured account of her life in Athens and Corfu, but he didn't listen either, he was far to engrossed in *Playboy* until she threw it across the room in exasperation. The chiropodist arrived and attached himself to Ivy who could hardly bring herself to speak to him. One by one, elderly gentlemen drifted in, but although they brightened after a drink and Berti, who had deserted the depressing Greek, made much of them, they might have been in their clubs.

'Did you see old Fred Knox has gone? It was in Tuesday's *Times*.'

'Yes, I was surprised, he was young to die, only seventy-six.' The old voices rumbled.

'I've changed to Unit Trusts, safe, you know, safe.'

And a voice broken by a cough said, 'Now I'm alone, I've bought an annuity.'

A rather querulous voice: 'Of course I'm lonely, bloody lonely, but I've this service room and there's always bridge.' They spoke amongst each other, occasionally giving Berti or Evelyn an affectionate pat as if they were dogs.

The atmosphere changed when three youngish men arrived. They were the ones who sometimes came to the house to laugh, but never went upstairs. They were accompanied by a woman wearing tight boots up to her knees; they had met her in a drinking club. She was a stocky, dark woman with a mass of frizzy hair, merry brown eyes and a pretty, tip-tilted nose, but an appallingly coarse skin under her heavy make-up. Berti, who was furious to see another woman had joined the party, seized one of the young men and started to dance. Everyone was suddenly shouting above the music, the old men clustering round the woman gate-crasher.

Evelyn, who was shrieking with laughter, had an arm round one of the young men and was adjusting his tie with the other, and a particularly drunk man had attached himself to Ivy. He was trying to tell her a horrible story about a strange woman who had come running out of a house and thrust a blue bird into his hand and asked him to wring its neck because it had broken its beak: 'What I want to know is do you wring a bird's neck to the left or the right? There I was with this bird in my hand and I didn't know. It was such a hot little bird, too. I put it in my pocket after killing it and it took a long time to cool down. Eventually I disposed of it by leaving it in a restaurant for a tip.'

Ivy backed away from him. 'Don't move, stay where you are,' she said as he made a grab at her, 'I'll get you another drink, whisky isn't it?' She snatched his glass and walked towards the bar, then made a dash for the door. Berti was well away, dancing by herself now and tossing off her clothes, and Evelyn, not to be outdone, was fumbling with the buttons of her black tunic. Ivy slipped away, feeling she had not left a moment too soon. Exhausted, she lay on her bed, fully dressed behind her locked door. She heard dreadful noises that came floating up the stairs, screams once, and later a violent ringing of the front door bell. Once there was a horrifying knocking and shouting outside her door and she recognized the chiropodist's voice, blurred with drink, asking to be let in. She lay there, shuddering, and eventually he went away.

The screams occurred when the despondent Greek slashed one of his wrists with a broken glass, then staggered about the room scattering blood. Berti and Evelyn first screamed in horror and later screamed to outdo each other. They were both afraid of blood.

Someone seized the Greek and forced him into a chair, his blood mingling with the crimson velvet seat and pouring down his purple-brown trousers.

Berti, who had stopped screaming, shouted, 'Hold his hand up, you fool, it'll stop the flow.' She stood there, practically naked, swaying, with her eyes on the bleeding man. Evelyn was being sick in a corner.

The gate-crasher, who had disappeared, returned with a pillow-case and a pair of nail scissors and proceeded to make bandages and, although she was far from sober, she bound the Greek's wrist in a professional manner, then telephoned for a taxi to take him to St George's hospital. Her efficiency had caused a curious silence to fall, only broken by faint foreign mutterings from the grey-faced man on the chair. Berti, with fumbling fingers, was slowly dressing and having a bewildered battle with the legs of her trousers. Evelyn lay full length on the sofa recovering from her sickness, and the men stood in a dejected group, with the exception of Jim Clarke, who had fallen asleep with his head resting on a table, oblivious to the fact that his hearing aid had fallen off and had been stamped into the floor. The poor man could hardly hear a thing without it; perhaps that was the reason he slept so soundly, dreaming of falling snow.

He failed to hear the heavy knocking and ringing of the bell which startled everyone into exclaiming, 'The taxi! No, it's the police.'

'A police raid!' the old man cried joyfully, 'I haven't been in one for years!' and he dived behind the curtains. Harry Rutter, bravely puffing out his chest, went to the door, to find an irate neighbour shivering on the doorstep in his pyjamas and dressing-gown. He had forgotten to put in his false teeth, but from the angry mumble emerging from his gums, Harry Rutter gathered what he wanted to convey, and patting him familiarly on the shoulder, assured him that he would be disturbed no more, the party was just ending and, profusely apologizing, steered him down the steps and out of the front gate.

When the expected taxi did arrive, there was some argument about who would accompany the wounded Greek to St George's. Most of the guests were not in a suitable condition and the ones that were decided it was time they went home. Harry Rutter, who seemed to have taken charge of things, was almost pressed into accepting; then, realizing that he would most probably have to pay for the taxi, backed out. The difficulty was solved by the woman gate-crasher offering to take him, and, as they drove off together, Berti said she expected she would have picked his pockets before they reached the hospital – and a good thing too.

The young men hurried to their car, dragging a drunken companion, determined to get away before anyone could ask them for a lift. One by one, the old gentlemen tottered down the steps and staggered into the cold night, some so unsteady they had to hang on to the railings from time to time. They waved their sticks in the air and called, 'Taxi, taxi,' but no taxis came and they trundled off towards the Boltons and Old Brompton Road.

Berti and Evelyn were left wandering among the dirty glasses and empty bottles, holding their aching heads. 'It stinks,' Berti said dejectedly. 'Help me to push up the window, dear. Oh, my God, what's this? They have left poor old Jim Clarke behind.'

7

It was Ivy's wedding day. She felt a wreck and she had forgotten to set her hair. It hung, damp and limp, round her pale face and she shivered after her lukewarm bath – the gas pressure was low that morning. She made herself a cup of tea and felt a little better, and then the thought that she had made an early appointment with her hairdresser penetrated her tired brain. Tying a headscarf over her straggling hair, she went downstairs, half expecting some left-over from the party to jump out on her. Except for the sound of Amy rattling the stove, the house was strangely quiet and Berti's door was firmly closed; it was usually left ajar so that she could call to people as they passed. The house smelt like a low-class pub, Ivy thought, and there was a queer sound coming from the drawing-room. Opening the door a chink, she peered into the reddish gloom of morning light filtering through the crimson curtains. An old man wrapped in an overcoat was snoring on the sofa. Perhaps he was dying and the snores were the death rattle. She hastily closed the door and left the house.

Downstairs, Amy stood drinking a cup of tea while

Hetty ate her breakfast and asked between mouthfuls, 'But what were they doing upstairs, Mummy? They were making the most fearful row and kept waking me up.'

Amy stirred her tea and said, 'The gas pressure is low this morning.'

'I dare say it is,' Hetty said crossly. 'But I want to know what the aunts were doing. You must have heard them.'

'Yes, of course. I think they were giving a wedding party for your Aunt Ivy, she's getting married this morning and I'm to be a witness. We are drinking champagne afterwards at the Rubens Hotel, just the four of us. Oh, I do hope my grey coat won't be out of place. It's really more of a tweed, but I've got a sweet little hat I bought at C & A and new suede gloves, although they are so expensive. I suppose I should have bought fabric ones. Hurry now, and don't forget to bring your school books back. You break-up today.'

She hustled Hetty out of the house and washed up the breakfast things and made the beds; it was some time before she could face going upstairs. Eventually, she carried up her cleaning things, took one look at the state of the drawing-room and carried them down again. 'They can't expect me to clean up all that mess, and an old man in there. Stains of blood all over the place and stinking of drink. Disgusting, I call it.'

She bolted the door at the top of her stairs and laid the clothes she intended to wear on her bed. Even the sight of the sweet little hat nestling on the eiderdown failed to cheer her. When she was dressed she heard a timid knock on the window and, drawing the net curtain slightly, she saw Ivy, all dressed for her wedding and carrying a small suitcase.

'Can I come in and phone for a taxi?' she whispered through the slightly open window. 'I dare not do it from the hall, although they seem to be sleeping, you never know with Berti.' Amy let her in and they huddled together by the warmth of the stove.

'Wasn't it awful last night? I'm not surprised you locked your door, Mrs Doll. And have you seen the drawing-room? There's an old man on the sofa giving a death rattle, or something horrible, amongst the empty bottles and I could swear I saw blood.'

Amy agreed on the awfulness of the previous night and tried unsuccessfully to telephone for a taxi, then offered to search for one in the street. It seemed unsuitable for a bride to find her own taxi. She put on her hat and left the house, Ivy calling from the basement steps, 'Find one quickly, dear Mrs Doll. I'd rather be early than late.'

She was waiting in the road when Amy returned, a watery sun shining on her newly-dressed, flower-scented hair. She darted into the taxi and, as it drove away, took a last look at the house. She saw Berti standing at an upstairs window, wanly waving.

'Poor old thing, what a wreck she looks! Thank God I've got away,' she said as she watched Amy gingerly forcing her work-roughened fingers into the new suede gloves. 'You won't forget that Carter Paterson are calling for my things on Monday? I couldn't face collecting them myself.'

Berti stood at the window, watching, until the taxi turned into the Boltons, glanced at her watch and said to herself bitterly, 'Damn little liar, told me she was to be at the registry office at twelve and it's not eleven yet. I bet she won't even ask us to Putney for a drink, although we went to all that trouble and expense to give her a farewell party.'

She fiercely attacked her crimson hair and rubbed lipstick into her tired cheeks. Then, with a shaking hand, she tried to outline her eyes with an eye-pencil. The point broke. 'Bloody thing, might have blinded me. Lord, I haven't had such a hangover for years,' she muttered, and held her aching head in her hands. When she felt a little better she staggered to the window and, after several efforts, managed to open it and reach for the half-empty milk bottle she kept there. Leaving the window open, she poured the milk into a tooth-glass and gulped it down with repugnance, then rinsing the glass in the wash-basin, she half-filled it with whisky, which she drank neat. Within ten minutes she was banging on Evelyn's door telling her to get dressed immediately and help clean the drawing-room. 'That bitch, Amy, has left a note in the hall telling us we must clean it ourselves, says it's in a disgusting condition.'

She charged into the drawing-room, pulled the curtains and revealed Jim Clarke sitting huddled up on the sofa holding the remains of his hearing aid in his papery old hands and looking at least a hundred years old.

'Good Lord, I'd forgotten you,' Berti said despondently. 'I think the hair of a dog's what you need.' Her eyes darted among the array of empty bottles and, finding one still containing a little Vodka, Berti poured it into a glass and held it to the old man's blue, unresponsive lips. She managed to force a little down his throat and smiled grimly at the idea of forcing a drink on Jim; perhaps it was the last he would ever have. She telephoned for a taxi to take him to the private hotel where he lived. 'Poor man, but I can't have him dying here and his son creating hell and perhaps an inquest.' She buttoned him into his overcoat, put his bowler hat square on his lolling head and supported him down the steps into the street where the taxi was already waiting, and with the driver's help packed him into it. His red-rimmed eyes had a bewildered expression; but he gave her a faint smile when she settled him comfortably in the seat and fumbled for her hand. She gave him a quick peck on the cheek and slammed the taxi door. Jim Clarke never visited the house in Mulberry Grove again.

Christmas Eve came and, with it, an official-looking letter for Berti. They had arranged their meagre collection of cards on the mantelshelf, three each so far. Last year Evelyn had been caught out sending cards to herself in a disguised hand and the show-down had been so terrible she had not dared do the same this year. She examined Berti's letter with envy. It had a solicitor's name stamped on the back and, knowing Berti's allowance was not due for another month, she thought it must be some Christmas bonus. She held it up to the light; but the envelope was thick and there was hardly time to steam it open because Berti might come back any minute. She was returning the hired record-player and collecting the deposit. After the expenses of the party, their finances were low and none of their men friends had been near them since. 'Ungrateful swine,' Berti called them as she staggered off with the heavy machine. 'And what are we supposed to do with the effing records, eat them?' Evelyn suggested giving them to Hetty for Christmas. 'But the child has no gramophone and, if she had, we don't want those Rocks and Stones coming up through the floorboards. Perhaps we could sell them as slightly shop-soiled.'

Berti returned, complaining of the cold and with five pound notes in her bag. 'Two pounds ten each, dear, and that's all I have to last me over Christmas. I don't know how I'm going to manage unless some manna falls from heaven. It sometimes does at this time of the year.'

Evelyn indicated the letter, flanked on either side by cards, and said, 'That looks hopeful; perhaps you have inherited a fortune.'

Berti scrabbled in her bag for her tinted bifocals and, taking the letter, studied the name on the back. 'It's my brother's solicitor,' she exclaimed hopefully. 'Perhaps he has had a fit of conscience and increased my allowance.' She went to the window to read the letter in the fading light. She read it through twice, folded it up very small and replaced it in its envelope, took off her spectacles and stared across the street.

Evelyn, burning with curiosity, cried impatiently, 'Well, what is it? Is it good news?' Berti appeared not to hear her and still stood with her back to the room, her eyes fixed on the damp garden; then she suddenly turned and walked out of the room without speaking. Evelyn sat fidgeting by the electric fire for over an hour, then went and knocked on Berti's door. There was no reply.

On Christmas morning Evelyn left the house early to spend the day with her relations at Twickenham. She knew she was unlikely to enjoy herself, but it was somewhere to go and they had given her a vague invitation. Berti would be completely alone unless Amy Doll took pity on her. When she returned in the evening the house was silent and Berti's door closed, so she decided she would wait until the morning to boast about the 'happy' Christmas she had had. In point of fact, she had been made to feel very unwelcome and it had been a miserable day.

The following morning, Boxing Day, Evelyn took Berti a cup of tea in bed 'to cheer her up' she said. Berti said she didn't need to be cheered up; but she drank the tea and listened to Evelyn's account of Christmas in Twickenham, the welcome she had received and the lavish food, the beautifully decorated table: 'They said they couldn't imagine Christmas without me. Oh, and I took a couple of those records for the children. I knew you didn't care for them.'

Berti chipped in, 'And what did they give you?'

'They gave me a set of buttons. Actually, they are not great present-givers. Hospitality's their strong point.'

Berti leant out of bed and put her cup on the floor and said brightly, 'I'd like to see those buttons. I might be able to give you some idea what to do with them.'

Evelyn sighed. 'Oh dear, I suppose I'll have no peace until you've seen them.' She went to her room and returned with a small cardboard box containing five mother-of-pearl buttons shaped like potato crisps. She held them out to Berti. 'Pretty, aren't they?'

Berti stirred them round with one long finger. 'But why only five?'

'Five! Oh yes, actually, my cousin lost one and they were too good to throw away, so she gave them to me.'

'Yes, I do see,' Berti went on relentlessly, 'do you know what I'd do with them if they were mine?'

'No, and I don't really want to know,' Evelyn quavered and held out her hand for the box.

'All the same, I'll tell you and I think you should take my advice. I'd throw them down the lavatory and pull the plug on them, even if they do stop up the drain. Second-hand buttons and not even a set!'

Evelyn snatched the box away and held it in both hands as if it contained something very precious. 'It's nice to be with one's family at Christmas,' she drawled. 'I suppose you had to spend it in the basement with the Dolls and that common waitress woman, Doris something,' and she darted from the room before Berti could reply.

Berti laughed as she got out of bed. 'Silly fool, with her rotten buttons. My cousins this, my cousins that. I bet they hate the sight of her.'

When she had bathed and dressed she went down to the basement to have a talk with Amy who was making a roly-poly pudding.

'Just a moment, Miss Berti, while I seal the ends. I'm baking it and don't want to lose the jam. It's more tasty baked. Hetty won't touch it boiled, says it's slimy and calls it slug pudding, the silly girl. Now, what was it you wanted to tell me?'

Berti looked down at Amy from her great height: her long jaw was trembling. 'To tell you the truth, Amy, I'm in a bit of a mess financially. My brother, the General, has died and they've stopped my allowance. The letter from the solicitor arrived on Christmas Eve and it has been weighing on my mind ever since. The other business isn't doing so well either, a seasonal depression, I believe it is called. I think I'll have to get a job. I worked for a time in a canteen for French officers during the war, you know. I'd like to do something like that again, but are there any French officers left now? One thing I can do, and that is to move into Ivy's little room; it's cheaper than mine. It will give that idiot, Evelyn, something to crow about but it can't be helped. Will it be all right if I move into it before the middle of next month? I'm paid up to the twelfth, I think.'

'Yes, Miss Berti, that'll be all right. I'm sorry about your brother, though. Is this the first you've heard of it?'

'Yes, although it must have appeared in the newspapers. The truth is I haven't seen or heard from him, except through his solicitor, for years. I'm the black sheep of the family and his ghastly wife wouldn't have me near the place. I was paid to keep away, I suppose. Poor old Martin, he was two years younger than me, and I remember, when we were very young, he used to cry at night and yell that there was a mouse in his cot, and one night our old nurse told him not to be so silly and pulled the bedclothes back and out jumped a mouse. I used to give him one of my supper biscuits to eat in bed and the crumbs must have attracted it. I adored him; but he grew up to be such a boring prig and went into the Army – did frightfully well, too. I wouldn't have known him if I'd met him in the street! Sad, really. I taught him how to ride a bicycle, and we used to fish together for those little things, minnows, I think they were called.' She absentmindedly picked up a small piece of dough and rolled it between her fingers. 'Years since I saw a roly-poly; I'd forgotten they existed. Well, thank you about the room, Amy. I think I'll go through my things and see if there is anything I can sell, my crocodile bag, for instance.' She trailed away.

Amy washed her floury hands, wrapped the roly-poly in silver foil and put it in the oven. 'It's worry, worry all the time,' she muttered as she sat dejectedly on a corner of the kitchen table. 'No more rent from Mrs Rope and now Miss Berti is playing me up, poor thing. I'll have to do something about letting the rooms and that means strangers in the house.' She left the table and went to open the back door for Hetty who came running down the steps, her face flushed from roller-skating round the square.

'I only fell down three times,' she cried breathlessly. 'An Indian boy helped me, he'd been given roller-skates too. I suppose he couldn't come to tea this afternoon? He's awfully well behaved, you'd like him.'

'I'll give you Indians,' Amy grumbled. Then, relenting, 'But I might take you to the pantomime this evening, that is, if I can get tickets.' Why sit at home, moping? she thought. Wait until the child went back to school and then see about getting new lodgers and solving the problem of the remaining old ones. Strange, Harry Lake had not been round for some time. Could he have lost interest in the case?

He appeared a few days later, carrying a large pink azalea in a pot, a belated Christmas present. He also brought a bottle of sherry, the real thing from Spain, which went down very well with the last of the mince pies. Hetty was in the upper part of the house helping Berti sort out her belongings, so he was alone with Amy and they sat either side of her round Victorian table sipping their sherry and nibbling mince pies. Amy, with her head on one side, listening to an account of his Christmas holiday at his parent's home in Leamington.

'My dad had this greengrocery business with a very good class of customer. Had it for donkey's years, but he's getting a bit past it now, so my brother, Ted, the one I'm living with, may go home and help him out. Mother's got her own little business. She doesn't go out to work or anything, but designs embroidery for women's magazines at home. You'd like her, she's awfully artistic, but jolly with it, always laughing. I wished I'd had a photograph of you to show her.'

'A photograph of me, to laugh at?'

'No, of course not; to show her how pretty you are. I tried to describe you but I'm no good at descriptions and all I could think of was that you looked like a rose.'

'A rose. What a lovely thing to say!'

'Well, it's true. I thought so the first time I saw you; that's why I came back to ask all those questions. I wanted to know about you and if you were married.'

Amy blushed and said in a low voice, 'And I was thinking you'd come to spy on me about the house and the goings-on upstairs.'

Mystified, he asked, 'What on earth do you mean? What goings-on upstairs?'

Amy shivered. 'You mean to say you don't know? Why, Harry, Mr Lake, I mean, all those old women upstairs are whores.' She pronounced it with the W.

'Wars? I don't understand.'

Tears streamed down Amy's cheeks. 'I expect I've said it wrong. What I mean is, that they are tarts and entertain old gentlemen in their rooms, for money. Isn't it awful?' and she put her head on the table and sobbed.

Harry Lake left his chair and stared down at Amy's heaving shoulders. 'I can hardly believe it. I thought they were a queer lot, but on the game!' And suddenly he was laughing, then he put his arms round Amy and drew her up from the table. 'Why, your face is all wet with tears, you silly little thing,' and he kissed her, first on the wet cheeks and then on the lips.

Later, over a second glass of sherry, Amy told him in detail how it had come about that her house had turned into a brothel almost overnight, when she had increased the rents. 'It was really the Señora who started it, although she was very discreet; but I think it's ending now, I really do. There's Ivy Rope married to a dentist and living in Putney and the Señora leaving to set up a little place of her own in Spain, and now Miss Berti's talking about getting a job, although goodness knows who would employ her. That only leaves Miss Evelyn and she wouldn't care to carry on on her own. At least, I don't think so.'

Harry bit into the last of the mince pies and munched it thoughtfully. 'Whatever they intend to do or not do, you must get them out of the house. Imposing on you like that! All the same, I can't help thinking it's the funniest thing that I have come across for years. Me coming into the house and all that going on upstairs. You kept well out of it, I hope.'

'Yes, Harry, I did. I bolted the door and kept the wireless on very loud.'

They heard the door at the top of the stairs open and uncertain footsteps descending. 'Hell, one of them's coming down now.' Harry jumped up to open the door. 'I'll tell them what I think of them, the dirty old bitches.'

In marched Hetty, draped in a black lace stole decorated with rusted silver medallions and wearing pointed green satin slippers on her feet. 'Do I look like the 1920's?' she laughed. Then she noticed Harry Lake standing by the door.

'Phew, you gave me quite a shock. I thought you were one of the ladies from upstairs,' he said and winked at Amy. He left a few minutes later. Amy accompanied him to the door.

When he had gone she stood remembering how it had been when she was in service and Alf Doll brought her home after an evening at the pictures. 'Why, I feel just as I used,' she thought, 'even if I am thirty-six and a widow. Has the sherry made me drunk, or is it really true?'

8

Jim Clarke never recovered from his last party. He had a stroke which partly paralysed him and was removed to an expensive home for incurable elderly people, where he was propped up in bed, day and night, his red eyes fixed on a picture on the opposite wall called 'The Piper of Dreams'.

Berti, wearing a skirt and a suitable face for invalids, visited him once a week, but she was not sure that he recognized her. She held his hand and talked to him brightly about things that had happened thirty or forty years ago; but, as no one had thought to provide him with a new hearing aid, it was unlikely that he heard. The nurses said he seemed happier after her visits, so she continued them in spite of the depression that they caused her.

One of her admirers had sent her a late Christmas present of five pounds. No one wanted to buy the crocodile handbag; but she had managed to sell a silver photograph frame and a cigarette-case for three pounds. She was reduced to smoking five cigarettes a day, which she re-rolled to turn into ten thin ones. Drink was a serious problem, so she cut out milk and her beloved whisky and relied on British sherry stretched with soda water. Fortunately for her, Evelyn was short of money and also drank British sherry, repeating from time to time that her father would turn in his grave if he knew what she was drinking, his cellar was famous throughout – er Devonshire.

'I thought you said your family seat was in Somerset,' Berti observed sharply.

'Our estates spread into the two counties,' Evelyn snapped as she tried to remember if Devonshire and Somerset were connected – or was there another county in between? She decided she must study the geography of south-west England in one of Hetty's school books at the first opportunity.

Early in January the Señora returned. The first evening Amy heard her three ladies assembled together in the drawing-room, waiting for their prey, she went upstairs and stood outside their room, listening for a few minutes to make sure they were alone, then gave a timid knock and entered. The Señora was bent over her embroidery; Berti was smoking one of her slender cigarettes and reading the classified advertisements in the *Evening Standard*, and Evelyn was painting her toenails in front of the fire. It was a peaceful, domestic scene.

Amy leant against the door, surveying her lodgers without speaking because she had forgotten her carefully rehearsed speech. At last she brought out: 'There's something I have to say to you. You won't like it, but I have had all I can stand with your gentlemen friends coming and going. That party was the last straw and no more men are going to come through my front door, so you will have to change your way of life, that's all there is to it. This was a respectable house until you dragged it in the mud and it's going to be respectable again.'

Berti interrupted with: 'But, Amy, I told you I was thinking of giving up my professional life and was looking for a job. I'm studying the market at this moment,' and she waved the *Evening Standard* so that sheets of newspaper fell about the floor.

Evelyn looked up from her magenta toenails in astonishment. 'You're decision is a bit sudden, isn't it? How do you think we'll manage when you have deprived us of our living?'

'I don't know and I don't care. I won't have you polluting my house any longer!' Amy cried wildly, and after rushing from the room, bolted herself in the basement. 'They can knock and bang and I won't answer,' she thought hysterically, 'and, if the worst comes to the worst, I'll get Harry to speak to them.' She felt the comfort, the blessed relief, of not being on her own anymore.

Upstairs, they sat with frozen faces. Berti broke the silence with: 'That bloody policeman has been talking to her. That's what it is.'

The Señora folder her embroidery, shrugged her impressive shoulders and said, 'I think I had better return to Spain immediately. There's no point in staying. A pity, I'd worked up such a nice little clientele.' She sighed and left the room.

Evelyn observed mournfully that Harry Rutter would be heart-broken. 'I don't mind losing the widower. Ivy was right: he is a pincher. But poor Harry! And there's Edgar, he is crazy about me.'

Berti snapped, 'If he's all that crazy about you he can take you to an hotel and pay for it. Stop talking all that blasted nonsense and face facts for once. You can't manage on your miserable three hundred a year, so you'll have to get work of some sort. Can you type, for instance? They are crying out for typists in the papers, copy typists, invoice typists; there's work for them all.'

Evelyn buckled her gold sandals and admired her toenails through the narrow straps. 'I wasn't brought up to be a typist,' she drawled affectedly.

Berti snorted. 'I wasn't brought up to do housework, you idiot, but I'm going to have a shot at it. Not live in, of course, but as a daily housekeeper to a bachelor, or perhaps a cook. Cooks seem to be paid more.'

'You, a cook! Why, you can't even open a tin.'

'I know, but with my intelligence I can soon learn. I'll start with roly-poly pudding; I helped Amy make one only the other day. Cooking's child's play with these modern ovens. Just a matter of numbers.'

'Harry might find you a job if I ask him. He is an expert on good food and has a lot of influence.'

'I'll find my own work, thank you,' Berti said coldly. She wished Evelyn would leave the room and give her a chance to telephone some of the advertisers for cooks. She felt strangely reluctant to apply with her listening; in fact, for once, she lacked self-confidence. Perhaps it would be better if she went to an agency. She had noticed a rather homely-looking one, with flower pots on the window-sill, in a nearby basement. Mrs Snell's, it was called, and, in spite of its humble appearance, women wearing expensive fur coats were constantly disappearing down the steps. On thinking it over, she decided she would try Mrs Snell's.

Evelyn dejectedly studied her toenails. The idea of working for her living appalled her. She remembered the dreary years of war when she had been forced to work in a food office – green books, blue books, buff books, points and clothing coupons. Anyway, who would want to employ her at her age, so lacking in experience and ability. There were Ivy's stories of haemorrhoids, tired legs and wool getting up her nostrils, and she was years younger. She tried to comfort herself with the thought that at least she still had her annuity and was not penniless like poor old Berti.

Wearing a brown tailored coat and skirt of rather old-fashioned cut, Berti sauntered past Mrs Snell's agency trying to summon her courage to descend the well-worn steps. A chauffeur-driven car drew up and disgorged a mauve-haired woman wrapped in mink. 'I'd die rather than work for her,' Berti thought. She was followed by a pretty but harassed young woman carrying a baby, with chubby boy twins toddling after her. She watched them make the perilous journey down the steps. 'Poor thing,' she thought, 'but I couldn't work for her with all those children, and there may be more at home. Someone should tell her about the pill.' Then a dark, foreign-looking couple went down, obviously 'married couple, no encumbrances'. The mauve-haired woman came up again like a fish coming up for air. The chauffeur carefully packed her into the car and they drove away. A middle-aged woman with frizzy brown hair, obviously a cook-housekeeper, bounced down the steps and Berti followed her.

The agency consisted of a wide passage, filled with people sitting on bentwood chairs, and an office. Mrs Snell, a bright little woman with too many teeth spilling out of her mouth, sat at a small desk, and at an even smaller desk her fat assistant sat, constantly answering the telephone. The employers sat in the office and the employees in the passage.

The harassed young mother was leaving as Berti entered the office and her parting words were: 'You will send someone, won't you? I'll wait in all day,' and the little family stumbled up the steps.

Mrs Snell said to her assistant, 'Make a note; if that deaf and dumb Dutch woman comes in, send her round.' Berti's confidence returned. If they were taking on deaf and dumb Dutchwomen, they ought to welcome her with open arms.

After an initial embarrassment caused by Berti being mistaken for an employer, the interview went well, although it necessitated some quick thinking and lying on Berti's part. As she had never been interviewed for a job before, she had no idea of the kind of questions she would be asked. Age, experience and references: every answer she gave was a lie. Eight years were knocked off her age; her experience consisted of years of cooking and housekeeping for her brother who had recently died; for a reference she gave Amy — an old family friend she had been living with since her brother's death. The interview over, she was asked to sit outside until she was called, and, with knees knocking more than usual, she joined the group in the passage and sank on to one of the bentwood chairs. An embarrassed silence descended and every eye was upon her. After about five minutes of small coughs and sighs, conversation started again.

A bleak-looking woman in dusty brown continued the same story she had been telling before Berti joined them: 'And as I was telling you, she only kept me the two days, so here I am, back again. Paid me the week, though. It was her cheek I didn't like: "I shan't be needing you after today. I've made other arrangements." She couldn't get me out of the house quick enough, although I'd done nothing wrong. Treated me as if I smelt or something.'

The frizzy-haired cook-housekeeper gave a downward smile. 'Oh, you meet some funny ones. People are very different in their own houses than to what they appear outside. Once they shut their front door on the street, their true character comes out. Those thin, dieting women are the worst. They're snarling with hunger, see, and take it out on the family and staff. I warn you all, keep clear of those starving women, choose the plump ones. There'll be better food in the house, too.' She looked down the line of seated figures and nodded her head several times.

Berti, who found it unbearable to be silent, said, 'Some people are born thin. Look at me and I don't diet.'

All eyes were turned on her and the housekeeper asked, 'But are you good-tempered?'

'No, of course not, I've a bloody awful temper.'

Someone tittered and the housekeeper frowned. 'That proves what I said. Thin women are not to be trusted.' She examined the foreign couple. 'Where are you from, Spain?'

Politely, but in halting English, the man, after glancing at his wife, as for permission, told her that they came from Portugal and had been in England for over a year, in private service. Now they were thinking of working at a school somewhere in the country. They were waiting to be interviewed. He added, 'But I would prefer to see a map first to know where we would be going.'

'You shouldn't pronounce it MAP, that's how common people speak. You should say MEP,' and, pursing her thin lips, the frizzy-haired woman repeated 'mep' several times.

The Portuguese gravely thanked her and said that in future he would remember to say 'mep'. Berti was opening her mouth to intervene when she was recalled to the office. A Lady Hooker had telephoned enquiring for a cook for six hours daily, three in the morning and three in the evening, no Sunday work, at a salary of six pounds a week. Lady Hooker was still on the telephone and her harsh voice could be heard vibrating through the instrument; could Berti go round immediately? Things were moving faster than Berti had intended; she had hoped for a few days' grace in which to study cookery. Reluctantly, she took a card with an address near Eaton Square written on it and left the agency. She stood in the street reassuring herself with the thought that, if she didn't like the job, she needn't take it. 'Six pounds a week seemed such a lot in the agency, but it's not much to live and drink and smoke on, and then there would be the fares; four journeys a day. I suppose there would be some meals included,' Berti said to herself as she absent-mindedly flagged a passing taxi. 'Hell, I didn't mean to do that,' she sighed. 'There's another three-and-six gone down the drain.'

The taxi drew up outside Monmouth House, an imposing block of flats with a doorman in livery standing outside. He opened the door for Berti and she walked in to a deeply-carpeted hall-lounge where women were sitting in haughty groups with disagreeable expressions on their faces; some were drinking coffee and slipping little white pellets into their cups. These must be the starving women she had been warned about. She scuttled towards the lift and was taken up to the sixth floor.

Even with the liftman's instructions she had some difficulty in finding Lady Hooker's flat. In spite of the spacious entrance hall, the building was a warren of overheated, narrow passages without windows that gave her a feeling of claustrophobia. When she found the door she was looking for, she stood outside for a moment, planning the lies she would tell and answering imaginary questions, her lips working. Then she pressed the bell. It was answered by Lady Hooker herself. She was a shark-like woman with snapping jaws and hard eyes; but she spoke to Berti quite pleasantly as she rushed her round the flat, a soulless place with cream-painted walls and furnished throughout with reproduction antique furniture. The kitchen was a shock, similar to the one Berti used at Mulberry Grove and the size of a second-rate lavatory, obviously only intended to be used for preparing simple breakfasts and snacks. Lady Hooker made the facial contortion that passed as a smile as she displayed it, then, quickly closing the door, she gave Berti a list of her duties.

'It's all frightfully easy really,' she said as she carelessly ran her fingers through her wiry black hair. 'You come here at eight – not before, though, eight exactly – and ask one of the porters to let you in. Then you prepare our breakfasts. We only have a simple meal, grapefruit and very thin toast for me and China tea with just a pinch of Indian, and my husband has cereal with warm milk – not hot, warm – and two eggs boiled for three minutes, no more, and Indian tea. He can't bear China. You see it's all frightfully simple and will only take you a matter of minutes to prepare. Now, come into the dining-room and I'll show you the linen we use.'

Berti followed her into the dining-room and Lady

Hooker started opening and shutting drawers in the imitation antique sideboard, pulling out various table clothes, napkins and a froth of lace mats. 'The green for breakfast, with these green paper napkins, and the lace mats with the matching napkins for dinner. The china and silver are kept in the bathroom cupboard, nowhere else to put them.' Another deprecating laugh. 'Now, what else is there to tell you; after breakfast you do the shopping and make some of the preparations for dinner, and there's coffee for my husband, Sir Godfrey; he likes it at eleven-thirty-seven, he's very particular about that. No housework, or course; that's all done by the staff. We hardly ever lunch at home; but we dine in most evenings and have a few friends round for bridge; simple meals of course, perhaps a little soup, fish followed by steak or cutlets and a savory or sweet. Of course, we never touch potatoes, so you won't have to bother about them. When we have finished dinner, you clear away, wash up and go home as soon as you like. The sooner the better for us. We can't stand kitchen noises; it puts us off our game.'

Berti agreed to start work the following Monday, which gave her three days in which to study cooking. As she was leaving, Lady Hooker said, 'I don't expect there will be a thing to eat in the house by Monday morning, so could you bring in a dozen best eggs and a couple of really large grapefruit, oh, and some bread if you can find a bakery open. Goodbye until Monday, eight o'clock exactly. Good morning,' the 'good morning' very drawn out.

Berti left Monmouth House in a state of exhilaration. 'There's nothing to it,' she thought as she darted through the traffic, searching for the King's Road, oblivious to cars' hooters and the screech of their brakes as she narrowly missed being run over. 'Any fool can boil an egg or grill a cutlet and, as for the puddings, I can easily knock something up.' When she found the King's Road she darted into a shop which sold plastic goods and came out with a frilly, pink apron. 'I must look the part,' she thought. 'I'll get a parlour-maid's cap and apron later. Cook's clothes are so dull, unless I wore a chef's hat, of course.'

Although she was tired when she got home — she had walked most of the way — she ran down to the basement, wearing her apron over her coat and skirt, and, flinging open the door, called, 'Amy, behold a working woman. I've landed a job as a cook, starting on Monday. Darling Amy, you will help me, won't you?'

Amy looked up from her ironing board. 'Do you really mean that, Miss Berti, about being a cook?'

'Yes, of course I mean it. Look, I've even bought an apron. Now, Amy, I'm really serious about this. What do you intend to have for luncheon today? You must let me cook it.'

'Oh, Miss Berti!' Amy protested miserably. 'I was only going to have meat balls and save a few for Hetty this evening. The meat and potatoes are cooked already and it's only a matter of mincing the meat.'

'Let me mince it,' Berti asked eagerly. 'Then I can stir it into the potatoes, squash it all into balls and cook them in some way. It will be an experience.'

Amy reluctantly disconnected her iron and produced the ingredients for making meat balls from the larder. Teaching Berti proved an exhausting business and it was three o'clock before they sat down to eat their burnt and withered meal. Berti planned to try her hand at chops in the evening.

9

At seven-thirty on Monday morning Berti was standing in a bus queue holding a plastic string bag containing a dozen best eggs, a small wrapped loaf and two large grapefruit. An icy wind blew round her stick-like legs; the queue was long and the buses infrequent, and it was ten minutes before she managed to board one, then it turned out to be a crawler. When she swore at the conductor he said, 'Keep your hair on, old girl, I could have you turned off for less.'

She arrived at Monmouth House shivering with cold and anger. As she hurried to the lift she felt hostile eyes boring into her string bag with its conspicuous groceries, and no one offered to open the lift doors for her. After some difficulty she found the Hooker's flat; then, remembering that on no account was she to ring the bell, she rushed about the passages to find a porter to let her in. She crept silently to the kitchen and put the kettle on to boil, then went into the dining-room muttering, 'Green table-cloth, with green paper napkins.' The only breakfast china she could find was old and chipped, the teapots stained and with broken spouts.

At eight-thirty exactly, Sir Godfrey rang for his breakfast and Berti pranced in wearing her pink apron and carrying the tray on one spread palm. She had rehearsed this carefully, having a professional eye on Sir Godfrey. Her hopes were rather dashed when she saw his bitter, white face bent over the *Financial Times*. He looked up from his paper and asked for All-Bran in a grating voice — 'and warm milk, if you please.' She tore back to the kitchen, leaving the door open, and hastily warmed some milk, then boiled the eggs counting sixty three times; her watch was in pawn. He was drumming one hand on the table when she returned, and complained about the door being left open.

At last she was free to start Lady Hooker's simple breakfast. Amy had shown her how to prepare grapefruit and, except for cutting a finger and making it a little bloody, she made quite a neat job of it. At nine Lady Hooker appeared, wearing a steel-grey negligee which added to her shark-like appearance. After breakfast she complained that the pinch of Indian in her tea had been too large and that the toast was hard and that Sir Godfrey's eggs had been slightly overdone.

When the complaints were exhausted she went on to discuss the evening meal: 'There will be four of us to dinner. As it is your first day, I want to make it easy for you, so we could start with smoked salmon, then some sort of soup — I leave that to you — then grilled cutlets served with cauliflower and béchamel sauce, followed by a cold sweet, a soufflé or mousse perhaps. Serve brown and white bread and don't forget to roll the butter. Oh, and the lemon. For heaven's sake don't cut it into those horrible round slices, cut it into four. That's all, I think. I must rush, I have an appointment with my hairdresser at eleven.'

Berti cried to the retreating grey back, 'But where do I shop and what about money? I shall need quite a lot; there's nothing in the cupboards and I'll have to start from scratch. There isn't even a shopping basket.'

Lady Hooker snapped round, looking fearfully shark-like. 'A basket!' She laughed scornfully. 'What would I know about baskets? Shop where you please and let me know how much I owe you at the end of the week.'

Berti gasped, then following Lady Hooker into the bedroom almost had the door shut on her indignant face. 'I'm sorry,' she exploded, 'I'm unable to finance your dinner party. I have very little money on me. Good God! If I could afford to buy smoked salmon I wouldn't be here.' She was vibrating with anger.

Lady Hooker, holding her fingers to her sallow temples with a pained expression, said, 'There's no need to get so excited, my good woman. Go and get the wretched stuff from Harrods on my account. Please allow me to dress or I will be late for my appointment.'

Berti returned to the kitchen and the washing up. If she went to Harrods immediately, would she return in time to make Sir Godfrey's coffee at eleven-thirty-seven? Should she return to the agency and tell them she couldn't work for Lady Hooker and ask them to find her something else? Still pondering, she put on her coat and gloves and went into the hall. A plump porter was strapping up a basket of laundry. He gave her a cheerful wink as she passed and she immediately felt better and winked back. She decided to stay for a week, collect her money, and in the meantime ask the agency to find her something else. After all, it was experience and she was bound to find it hard at first.

She came out of Harrods laden with food. She had paid for the bread and some of the smaller items herself because she could hardly ask to have them put on the account. She must remember to ask for the money for all these odds and ends at the end of the week. Clutching her packages, with a milk bottle sticking out of one pocket and her chin pressed on a cauliflower to prevent it falling, she arrived at Monmouth House. The commissionaire opened the door with a disgruntled expression on his face. Perhaps she should have used some service entrance. In the dining-room she could see waiters hovering over tables and the lounge was filled with people, mostly women, who fixed their glittering mascara-ed eyes on Berti. She threw back her head with a haughty gesture and the cauliflower shot across the carpet, followed by a lemon. A ferocious porter took her packages from her and dumped them in the lift while she retrieved the cauliflower and lemon. 'Perhaps I'll be able to laugh at this one day,' she thought miserably as she entered the lift with the cauliflower held in front of her like a bouquet. Except for Sir Godfrey becoming fretful over his coffee being slightly delayed the rest of the morning passed peacefully and she left with her confidence slightly restored.

When she returned to Monmouth House in the evening she was wearing a hat and completely different clothes and managed to get through the hall unrecognized, although she was carrying a large round tissue-paper-covered parcel tied with a blue bow. It contained a chocolate mousse kindly made by Amy Doll in her best cut-glass bowl.

As she was laying the dining-table with lacy mats and napkins Lady Hooker came in with a glass of sherry in her hand. Her black hair was set in a highly-lacquered helmet and her face appeared more relaxed.

'You have laid the table very nicely,' she said brightly,

'except for the glasses; we'll be drinking champagne. Now, you'll be able to manage the waiting, won't you?'

'Wait at table?' Berti squawked. 'Not if I'm to do the cooking. I'm not a bloody robot. Get someone from downstairs to do it.'

'Oh, well, if you feel like that about it, just put the food on the table and clear away the dirty plates between courses. Frightfully uncivilized. I took it for granted you'd wait.'

Berti asked why she bothered with dinner parties when there was a perfectly good restaurant downstairs.

Lady Hooker flashed her shark's teeth and screeched, 'My dear woman, if you knew the prices they charged. It's quite out of the question.' She watched Berti carry the best china from the bathroom to the kitchen with a penetrating eye as if willing her not to break it. 'You will take care of it, won't you? I've had this dinner service for twelve years and nothing has been broken so far. By the way, do remember to keep the kitchen door closed. I don't want cooking smells to escape into the hall, so unpleasant.' She wandered off to change, leaving Berti in the wretched·little kitchen with the door closed to concentrate on her cooking.

The soup was easy; packet asparagus with chopped spring onion to disguise it and grated cheese to sprinkle in at the last moment. Amy had provided the onion and grated cheese. The cauliflower was too large for the saucepan, so she halved it. The chops, which were unusually thick and clumsy-looking, wouldn't fit under the grill and had to be cooked in the dirty little oven, and every few minutes she opened the door to see what was happening to them. The kitchen became so over-heated that even the cold-water tap ran hot. Her face, usually so pale, became red and swollen. She tried opening the door a chink, but after a few minutes found it closed again.

With sweat running down her burning cheeks she suddenly had an oasis-like vision of her mother's kitchen as it had really been, not as she so often described it, with chefs, butlers and footmen falling over each other. She closed her eyes and remembered the long, rather dark room with its many cupboards, the blackleaded range with its shining steel fender, the enormous dish-covers hanging from the walls, the Windsor chairs – the ones with arms and red cotton cushions on the seats – and the two maids floating biscuits in their dark brown tea, gossiping about the Master and the Mistress and Miss Ball the governess, who wore dusty pink and gave the children Beecham's pills on Saturday night to clean them out for Sunday. She remembered her mother wearing an enormous white apron, instructing the younger maid, Nelly, in the art of making pastry – apple pies with china funnels in the centre – and dripping toast suppers sitting on the kitchen fender, her brother in his camel-hair dressing-gown, with his hair still damp from his bath, hesitantly reading *Martin Rattler* to her between mouthfuls.

Gasping, she opened the door and took a few breaths of the central-heated air, which seemed as refreshing as a mountain breeze, hastily closing it again when she heard the bell ring. Welcoming sounds penetrated her private furnace: Sir Godfrey had actually laughed. She imagined them enjoying their pre-dinner drinks in anticipation of a well-cooked meal while she struggled with her second attempt at béchamel sauce. At seven-forty-five she lit the candles on the dining-table, served the soup, creamy white with flecks of green, and rang the little silver bell. When she returned to the kitchen she saw the wilting smoked salmon and had a sinking feeling that it had been intended for the first course. Nevertheless, she had a feeling of achievement as she poured the not-so-lumpy sauce over the cauliflower and garnished the thick cutlets (or were they chops?) with watercress.

At last it was time to take the coffee into the drawing-room, then all that was to be faced was the mountain of washing up stacked around the tiny sink and on the floor. As she was clearing the table in the dining-room she could hear party conversation and laughter through the folding doors. 'But, Nora,' she heard, 'why do all your cooks have such red faces? Do they drink or something?' Then she caught, 'Said she wasn't a bloody robot. What we have to put up with!' The dish-washing seemed to go on for hours.

Once, Lady Hooker put a querulous face round the door and snapped, 'Don't take all night, but do take care of my china. From the noise you're making I'm sure you are chipping it.' Berti was too exhausted to reply.

While Berti was bent over the sink of Lady Hooker's appalling little kitchen, Amy and Harry sat side by side, talking, in the Mulberry Grove basement.

'Have you sent the old girls packing yet?' Harry asked as he put his arm round Amy's waist.

'More or less, Harry,' she whispered timidly. 'The Señora is leaving at the end of the month so there will only be the two, and I was waiting until they were fixed up with suitable jobs. Miss Berti has started as a cook to a titled lady; but I don't know how long it will last, although I've taught her quite a lot in the last few days. Miss Evelyn was talking about starting something called a charm school; but I told her I'm not having any of that nonsense, even if her father was a bishop, which I very much doubt. She could go into the haberdashery like little Mrs Rope, Mrs Thomson, I should say. Did I tell you? They are off to Canada a fortnight today and seem ever so happy together.'

'Yes, you mentioned it before. What I'm worried about is those two skinny ones in trousers. We don't want to be landed with them. I was thinking we'd move upstairs after we were married and let this basement to someone from the station. I'll do the whole place up for you, Amy dear, wallpaper the lounge. Why, you won't recognize it upstairs when I have had a go at it — contemporary, that's what it will be; but we don't want those old women flitting about like bats in a belfry.'

Sleet was falling when Berti left the house for her second day of work. Remembering the struggle of the previous morning, she walked to Gloucester Road and took the underground. She fought her way into the train by kicking with her long, pointed shoes. London's early morning battle for transport was something she had never met before. Exhausted but warm, she left Sloane Square Station, but by the time she reached Monmouth House she felt numb with cold and icy tears were running down her cheeks. Looking through her tears at a nearby clock she saw, to her horror, that she was twelve minutes early. She tried pacing up and down in front of the building until the cold drove her in and she sat thawing in the empty lounge. When she saw a hall porter bearing down on her, she shot into the lift and walked about the passages with a purposeful air until she judged it was time to find someone to let her into the flat. She came across the same cheerful porter who had winked at her the previous day.

As he fitted the key into the door he said, 'How are you getting on, dear? Find her a bit of a Tartar, eh?'

'How long do her cooks usually stay?' Berti asked in a low voice.

He shrugged his shoulders and laughed. 'You're not doing so badly. Some only last a morning. One did stay a month, a foreigner, but it ended in the hell of a row.'

Berti went despondently into the kitchen and started to prepare Sir Godfrey's breakfast. As she laid the table she said, 'There's your blasted green table-cloth and here's your effing All Bran and, when you ring your horrid little bell, you'll be lucky if I don't throw your soft-boiled eggs at your blasted head.' Slightly relieved, she returned to the kitchen and poured herself a cup of tea from Sir Godfrey's pot. No sooner had she taken it into the dining-room with the three-minute eggs than he rang the bell again and asked in his grating voice for his green paper napkin. Vibrating with anger, she took one from the nearby sideboard drawer and put it beside his plate and walked slowly back to the kitchen. Her legs ached from the unaccustomed hours of standing and there was no room for a chair in the kitchen.

Listlessly she prepared Lady Hooker's breakfast. Lady Hooker ignored her when she took in the tea, grapefruit and toast. Obviously she was displeased with the previous evening's dinner. Later, when she went to clear away, she found two of the women staff had taken over the flat, one using an electric carpet-sweeper and the other flicking with a feather duster. Lady Hooker had retired to her bedroom.

One of the maids said, 'New, aren't you?' and giggled. She had a strong Irish accent and legs with fat calves, the kind that bulge over high-laced boots. 'Do you dye your hair or is it natural?' she asked with another giggle, echoed by the girl with the feather duster. Berti ignored them and marched into the kitchen with the tray.

While she was bent over the low sink, Lady Hooker opened the door and said, 'I shall be out until this evening and there are several things I want to say before I leave. One thing I must tell you, I wasn't at all pleased with the dinner last night. I was so ashamed when those dreadful chump chops appeared on the table when I'd ordered cutlets. Surely you know the difference between chump chops and cutlets? Then the cauliflower, it was halved, a cauliflower should always be served whole. Any idiot knows that. The soup and mousse were passable, but that frightful glass bowl; where on earth did you find it?' She glowered at Berti from under a fur toque. 'I hope you will do better this evening. There will be four to dinner and I particularly want everything to be perfect. I'll leave the soup to you. Then we'll have sole *à la Reform*, steak served with mushrooms and peas, and – what about pancakes? We like them served with lemon and very crisp. Be careful how you lay the table, clean napkins and cloth of course, and we'll be drinking claret.'

Wearily Berti asked if she was to use the account at Harrods again.

'Do you mean to say you have again come without money? In that case, I suppose you'd better go to Harrods but I don't like to think of my account mounting up like this. I told you I'd settle up with you at the end of the week.' Lady Hooker got as far as the front door, then returned to the attack. 'You won't forget Sir Godfrey's coffee at eleven-thirty-seven, will you? And do your best with the dinner this evening. Chump chops!'

It was the thought of sole *à la Reform* that decided Berti – she must leave Monmouth House and never return. She ate the remains of the chocolate mousse, washed the bowl and carefully wrapped it in its tissue-paper and tied it with the blue ribbon. She waited for ten minutes to make sure she didn't run into Lady Hooker, then left the flat as if on her way to do the shopping. She marched through the lounge, where women were already sitting over their coffee, waited for the disapproving commissionaire to open the door for her, and swept into the icy street. 'Thank heaven, I'll never see that woman again,' she thought, then suddenly doubled up with hysterical laughter, thinking of her returning a few minutes before her dinner party to find nothing prepared. She would have to take her guests down to the restaurant and spend pounds. Then the image of the skinny and bleak-faced Sir Godfrey expecting his coffee at eleven-thirty-seven on the dot and ringing his little silver bell, made her laugh again.

Later, struggling against the bitter wind, she realized how out-of-pocket she was; all that slavery and nothing for it, the dozen best eggs, grapefruits and other items. There was a list of them in her bag. When she reached Mulberry Grove there would be Amy to face and, far worse, Evelyn. In spite of the intense cold and her aching legs she walked home; she felt too dazed to cope with London transport. When she reached the front door her hands were so chilled she couldn't get at her key, one arm was completely numb from clutching the glass bowl, so she pressed the bell with her elbow.

Evelyn, still wearing her dressing-gown and her hair in rollers, opened the door and, laughing, said, 'Got the sack already, Berti? I knew they'd never stand your cooking.'

'No, they didn't sack me, I've resigned. I don't feel very well, 'flu or something. Could you bring me a hot-water bottle,' and she slowly went upstairs, still clutching Amy's glass bowl in her frozen arms.

She lay in bed, shivering and muttering to herself, 'Why did I let that bitch bully me? I should have thrown her blasted china at her face and then stamped it into the ground. Chump chops! I'd like to choke her with chump chops.'

Evelyn drifted in from time to time and talked about opening a charm school. 'I'd teach the girls how to dress and undress gracefully and improve their minds by taking them round museums, and then there's my French.' Evelyn went on and on with her nonsensical plans while Berti lay in bed, too ill to make the effort to tell her what a bore she thought her. She lay shivering, yet burning, and, when Evelyn gave her a hot lemon drink, her teeth rattled against the glass. Becoming alarmed, she asked Amy to send for a doctor.

During the night she became delirious, calling out a jumble of names and mumbling that she was shut in a burning kitchen; 'Open the door, for Christ's sake open the door,' she pleaded. Amy sat with her all night and when the morning came Berti seemed calmer, but weak, and having difficulty with her breathing. When the doctor came he said she was suffering from pneumonia in both lungs and was in a poor state of health generally. It was going to be a long business.

Berti was confined to her bed for over three weeks, Amy and Evelyn taking turns to nurse her and Amy paying for expensive drugs and the doctor's bills to face. Berti's hair grew long and wispy down her neck, half white, and half red, and, with her sunken cheeks, she resembled a consumptive eighteenth-century poet. When her illness was at its height she became unusually docile, begging Amy not to let her die. She rambled about her life as a child, picnics in bluebell woods, drinking musty-tasting tea from a Thermos flask. 'But the honey sandwiches were delicious. Can I have a honey sandwich, Amy? Real honey, not that stuff in jars.' Once, she clutched Amy's arm, entreating her to believe that someone called Charlie Fox had shot himself because of her. 'You do believe it, don't you, Amy?' she pleaded. Amy said she did and that it was very remiss of him to kill himself like that. 'Oh, he didn't die. Missed death by half an inch, they told me. Think how he must have loved me. But spiteful people said he had money worries.' One night she confessed to having had three abortions and wondered if it would count as a sin if she died.

Amy was deeply shocked, but she said, 'It depends on how you look at it, dear. The laws have changed now and even school-girls have them on the National Health.'

Once it was sweet peas she wanted. She cried for them one night after some dream that had disturbed her. 'I'd forgotten how they smelt. Why didn't someone remind me? Now it's too late and I'll never smell them again.' In the morning, Amy combed the shops for sweet peas, but it was February and there were none. Perhaps it was just as well, because when she returned it was something called 'sailor's crab' Berti was crying for.

When Berti began to recover it was found she had lost the use of one arm; it was drawn up and the hand claw-like. With convalescence she became appallingly bad-tempered, swearing and shouting – 'Blast you, why can't you shut the door? Do you want to kill me?' and calling Amy's carefully prepared meals 'filthy muck'. She accused the doctor of smoking while he examined her and 'using my navel as a bloody ash-tray.' The poor man had only smoked a cigar at home before setting out on his rounds, and Amy was rather proud of having a doctor who smelt of cigars and not disinfectant. The doctor laughed and prescribed small doses of barbitone to calm her down. Amy and Evelyn thought the doses were too weak because they made little difference.

Evelyn, who had nursed Berti with a devotion that surprised Amy and the Señora, was now hurt by Berti's ingratitude. 'She called me a crashing bore with the face of a prawn and the brains of a louse,' she complained to Amy tearfully. Nevertheless, she still continued to do her share of nursing Berti and bought her the little delicacies she craved; one day mushrooms and another celery hearts. She had the cravings of a pregnant woman, but could often only swallow a few mouthfuls of the food she begged for. As she recovered she began to worry about Jim Clarke and asked Evelyn to telephone the nursing home. When she did so, they told her he had had another stroke and was now completely paralysed and knew no one.

After being confined to her room for nearly a month, Berti tottered downstairs and sat huddled in front of the drawing-room fire. She wore a purple headscarf to cover her piebald hair and had put lipstick on her lips and hollow cheeks. She resembled a painted corpse. It was her sixty-fifth birthday, but she looked and felt ten years older, had lost the use of one arm, and had one-and-fourpence in her bag to last her for the rest of her life.

* * *

Evelyn, at last free to leave the house, was lunching with Harry Rutter whom she still occasionally met, although he was barred from Mulberry Grove. If Amy or Harry Lake saw any of the old clients coming through the gate, they politely sent them away, and soon they ceased to come. One night the front garden was invaded by a party of young men with bottles in their hands.

Their laughter woke Amy and she rushed out in her dressing-gown, waving the rake from the Aga above her head in a threatening manner. 'They don't live here any more. Get out before I call the police,' she commanded and, to her amazement, still laughing, they left. She returned to the basement and was violently sick in the passage. At last, the nights were quiet and the iron gate of the front garden squeaked and banged no more.

While Evelyn lunched with Harry Rutter, Berti sat depressed and alone in the drawing-room. She brightened when Hetty came in with her luncheon on a tray, steamed fish with parsley sauce and a bowl of prunes. She arranged it neatly on one of the little gilt tables and drew up a chair for Berti who complained, 'Only fish, I'd have enjoyed grilled gammon. Prunes! Take them away, child, they remind me of cockroaches. What's that bloody great book under your arm?'

Hetty held the heavy book out for Berti to see. 'It's *Anna Karenina*. I took it from the free library to do exercises with, to develop my bust, you know. Then I started to read it and it's wonderful – the first novel I've enjoyed. I've had it out three times. Wouldn't you like to read it? Look, it's illustrated.'

Berti waved the book away. 'I don't want to see it. I read it in French when it first came out.'

'Did you?' Hetty idly turned the pages. 'It says here, it was first published in 1876.'

Berti snapped, 'I don't care when it was published. You can go downstairs now and take the prunes with you.'

Eating the prunes with her fingers, Hetty went.

IO

Harry Lake was there the day the Señora left. He helped her down with her heavy luggage, which in her excitement she called '*equipaje*,' and offered her his handkerchief to wipe the tears that poured from her thickly mascara-ed eyes. Berti stood at the window, waving with one long pointed hand, the other held limply to her chest like a bird's claw. Evelyn skipped about the pavement in purple trews that had not been paid for yet. It was years since she had travelled and the thought of the Señora's journey excited her.

Amy patted the Señora's hand and told her how much she would miss her. Actually, all she felt was relief, and, as the taxi drove away and the Señora's kisses were still wet on her cheeks, she turned to Harry, laughing, and said, 'That's another of them gone.' Evelyn was posed at the corner of the square waving a chiffon scarf, hoping she looked as if she was launching a thousand ships.

Down in the basement, Harry said, 'Well, we've got six weeks to get rid of the other two in. It won't be so difficult with old Purple-pants; the other one's the problem. I told you you'd get landed with her.'

Amy sighed and examined her clean but work-worn hands. At last she said, 'I can't turn her out, Harry. Wait a week or two until she's stronger, then we'll see about it. Perhaps her family would do something. I could make some enquiries, then write and tell them the position. You'll help me with the letter, won't you?'

'Yes, of course, Amy love. Have you mentioned it to Hetty yet, about us getting married?'

Amy flushed and said she hadn't quite got round to it but she thought the child had guessed something. 'But I'm worried about her, Harry. She's started playing truant again. She's been so much brighter lately, taking an interest in her appearance and all, and now this truant thing has returned. I thought she'd grown out of it. And there's something queer going on. Two of my best blue plates missing, Blue Dawn they're called, and now there are only four instead of six. Tinned salmon's missing and cornflakes. That headmistress telephoned for me to go and see her, but I said there was illness in the house. I don't want to have to face her again. Do you think it would be a good idea if you followed the child on one of your free mornings, that is, if you can spare the time?' she asked shyly.

'I suppose so,' he agreed, without enthusiasm. He picked up a copy of Amy's favourite woman's paper. 'If you don't mind me saying so, I think you've brought up the girl to be too old-fashioned. Look at all these teenage kids, as bright as buttons, dressed in something they call weekend gear. And have you seen their bed-rooms? Look at this one, more like a sitting-room with its divan and built-in furniture. "A with-it room for a swinging girl", it says here. What about me making a room like that upstairs? A place she can bring her friends to and she could have a gas-ring up there so that she can make tea or coffee. I glanced in her room the other day and saw a white iron bed stuck in the middle and nowhere to hang her clothes except behind a dark old curtain, a mirror she can only see her head in, perched on a chest of drawers, and a great pile of musty old *Punches* and such-like, stacked against a wall. The fish are nice, though, and that's what made me go in and have a look round. The poor kid's years behind the times.'

'Yes, I expect you're right, dear; but it's better to be a little backward than too forward. You know what these teenagers are, sex-addicts, and I don't know what. I agree about the room, it's a lovely idea if it doesn't cost too much.'

'Don't worry about that. I'll provide all the materials for the job and you just do the trimmings, curtains and things. If the coast's clear, let's go upstairs and decide which room she's to have.'

In a garden in Holland Park, Hetty smashed two blue plates, then hammered them into small pieces with a stone and handed them to Glover, who was bent over his mosaic.

'Do you think the pale-blue next to the gold and the darker for the edges, or the other way round?' he asked as he straightened his aching back. 'The dark would act as a sort of frame, don't you think?'

Hetty agreed and said she hoped the two blue plates would provide enough light-blue to surround the chalice. 'If I take any more, my mother's bound to notice. How did you manage to get all that dark-blue? Could you spare some for me?'

'Of course, my dear Hester. I was very fortunate, you know, and managed to make off with the china umbrella-stand and it hasn't been missed yet. I've got my eye on some rather attractive deep pink cups at the back of the china cupboard. We haven't used them for years and they have such beautiful golden rims. I do like gold in my designs. I'm not really happy about using toffee papers. Quite effective on this chalice, I suppose, but slightly vulgar, don't you agree?'

'I suppose so,' Hetty said doubtfully. 'You must have eaten an awful lot of toffee to collect all that paper.'

'Indeed I did. I've put on pounds. My family are astonished at my passion for toffee. There's still some paper left if you want it for that bowl of fruit you're working on. Come in useful for the bananas.'

A thin grey cat appeared, weaving its way through the long grass. When it reached Hetty it rubbed itself against her legs, purring with a worn old purr. Hetty rummaged in her satchel and produced a tin of salmon, then went to the summer-house, the cat running ahead with it's shabby tail held high. There was a tin-opener, some plastic bowls and a packet of cornflakes on the window-sill and she prepared the cat's meal, mixing salmon with the cornflakes. Then she poured more of the cereal into a separate bowl. 'I'm afraid that'll have to last you until I come on Saturday,' she said regretfully, looking down at the poor, half-starved creature crouched over its food. In a box in a corner, curled up on one of Amy's best Shetland vests, there were three kittens, with their eyes just beginning to open. One of them was pure white and she decided that, as soon as it was old enough, she would somehow manage to smuggle it home. When it became an established fact, surely her mother wouldn't turn it out. She had examined the kittens carefully to determine their sex, but they all seemed the same. She thought, if she called her kitten

Prince, her mother would take it for granted that it was a tom-cat; but her secret name for it would be Vronsky.

When she returned to the garden, Glover was standing looking down at his morning's work with a satisfied expression on his face. 'It's the best I've done so far,' he said happily. 'Tell you what, Hester, I'll take you out to lunch. My mother and· sister, Agnes, are away from home today and Mother gave me a pound to spend. A pound would be plenty for both of us and leave some change, I should think. I do like a little to rattle in my pockets.'

They cleaned their hands on the damp grass, smoothed their hair with their fingers and walked in the direction of Shepherd's Bush, where there was an Italian restaurant where they occasionally ate when Glover was in funds. They both had a passion for spaghetti. On their way, they stopped to look in shop windows from time to time. There was an extremely small shop where antique jewellery was sold that appealed to them very much, and for some strange reason Glover always insisted on crossing the road to a shoe-menders where he could watch the cobblers working. Hetty did not care for the smell that came through the open doors and stood a little way away, ready to dodge into the shop if any of the girls from her school appeared. Near the restaurant there was a tobacconists which had a small display of old pipes in the centre of the window. The bowl of one of the pipes was carved to represent an Indian's head with a feathered headdress and another was a skull. Glover had been longing to buy the pipe with the Indian's head for years, although he did not smoke.

A slight disadvantage about eating spaghetti with Glover was the mess he made of it. Hetty had to eat with her eyes cast down; but, when their plates were empty, she looked up and said breathlessly, 'Do you know, I think my mother is going to marry a policeman.'

A wary look came into Glover's innocent blue eyes. 'A policeman, did you say? I was afraid of policemen when I was a child. Of course, I'm not afraid of them now. I know servants say silly things to children; all the same, I think your mother should choose someone else to marry, a soldier or sailor for instance.'

Hetty laughed. 'I don't think she knows any, but this policeman seems all right, not very policey. He does our garden for us. Mother needs someone to look after her, she's so timid. She's scared stiff of the aunts who live with us and my headmistress makes her tremble like a jelly. Oh, that reminds me. Will there be enough for a pudding or ice-cream?' They studied the menu carefully, adding up how much the food they had already eaten cost, and were relieved to discover that even with large ice-creams there would still be change for Glover's pockets.

When they finished their meal Glover studied his nickel watch with cowboys painted on the face and said there were over two hours before they need return to their homes. 'What about the Science Museum?' he suggested hopefully. 'There'd still be time to see those Victorian dolls you're so keen on.' He took up his gloves, which were hanging over the back of his chair, and, slinging them round his neck, waited for Hetty's decision.

'Yes, of course we'll go to the Science Museum,' she agreed politely, 'and after the dolls, if there's enough time, we could walk round Harrods and sit in the bank for a bit.'

When they left, the waitress frowned as she cleared the table and saw her twopenny tip. 'Mean old loony,' she muttered, 'only left twopence and smeared tomato sauce all over the cloth.'

That evening, Berti telephoned the nursing home where Jim Clarke lay and they told her that he had died three hours ago. Amy was talking to her friend Doris and did not hear Berti's anguished scream.

Doris loosened her suspenders before she sat down. 'My stockings go so quick if I put any strain on them; my legs must be getting fat or something. Perhaps I ought to take to garters, only they say they're bad for the veins.' Seated comfortably, she continued with an arch look, 'And how are you getting on with your policeman friend? Find the nights warmer now the spring's coming on?'

'Not particularly. Basements are inclined to be cold, you know.' Then Amy's longing to confide overcame her. 'I'll let you into a secret: Harry and I plan to marry at Easter and move upstairs. We're going to make Hetty a swinging bedroom, I think swinging was the word, anyway a modern bed-sitting room with a divan and built-in cupboards and a bookcase, a nice place where she can entertain her friends and play records. Harry thinks I've brought her up too old-fashioned.'

'I'll say you have, poor kid. Does she still play truant?'

Amy sighed. 'Yes, I'm afraid she does. It's all started up again now the weather's changed for the better. I've asked Harry to follow her to find out what she gets up to. I can't let it go on or she'll be turned out of the school. This should be a happy time for me but I've got so much to worry about, what with Hetty and those two upstairs and Miss Berti's illness. I must say she looks a wreck and one of her arms is drawn up in a horrible way.'

'Oh, well, we all have our troubles. Did I tell you, a man fell off our roof the other day? Fixing an aerial, he was. They were covering him with a cloth when I came home and he was lying underneath as dead as a doornail. Do you remember poor Mother committing suicide? That was a shock, I can tell you. She was at the change and the sheets went yellow and she hung herself one Monday. It was the sight of clothes hung acoss the back yard for all to see that did it.'

'As if I could forget a thing like that. But your mum always was a bit strange. Always at the sterilizer and I seem to remember she kept leeches in a jar on the window-sill and fed them with raw meat once a week. Or is that someone else I'm thinking of?'

'No, that was Ma all right. They came in useful when friends had boils. She came from the country, that's all that was wrong with her. Making jams and bottling fruit and the place full of wasps. But she was good to me when I had Solly, you must admit that.'

'Indeed she was. Never reproached you, did she? I didn't mean to criticize your mother, you know that. Do you remember Dad's dairy with a slot for pennies in the door? You put your penny in and the milk came gushing out. You don't see anything like that now. It wouldn't be considered hygenic.'

'There were two great china storks in the shop window. I wonder what happened to them.'

'They were put in the sale before the dairy was pulled down. A pity, I could do with them in the garden here. Fetched practically nothing.'

'I say, where's Hetty this evening? Solly's bound to ask after her when I get home.'

Amy froze. 'She's gone to a concert with her school, at the Albert Hall, if you please, and the ticket seven-and-six.' She left her chair and made for the scullery, saying over her shoulder, 'She'll be home in a minute. Must warm up the shepherd's pie for the child.'

Doris bent down and attached her flopping stockings to her suspenders. She knew when she wasn't wanted.

Berti was alone when she heard that Jim Clarke was dead. No one heard her scream, she might as well be dead herself for all they cared. She paced up and down the room with her close-legged walk, clawing at her neck with her good hand. She stopped in front of the mirrors and studied her reflection, feeling slightly exhilarated when she saw her sorrowful face. 'We lived together for five years, three in Ostend, one in Athens — filthy hole, I can't remember what we were doing there. Then that unforgettable year in Corfu. Why, it's almost like losing a husband, a tragedy really.'

She wandered to the drink cupboard without much hope. All it contained was half a bottle of sherry. She struggled to remove the cork with one hand, eventually using her teeth. As she poured the dark, sweet liquid into a glass she thought, 'Jim wouldn't like to see me drinking this muck.' She tried to remember why they parted: did she go off with Cocky or did Jim go off with that low-class Australian girl with red hair? She seemed to remember a frightful quarrel and hurling suitcases through a hotel window. Still, he had been part of her life, and they had linked up again a few years ago after a chance meeting in the Hoop and Toy near South Kensington Station; and now he was dead. She choked over her sherry, decided she couldn't stand her own company any longer and trailed downstairs to harass Amy.

Evelyn finished her plate of chicken sandwiches and bent to select a chocolate from the box beside her. She was sitting in an arm-chair in front of an electric fire and as she ate she read the latest number of *Nova*. She had not felt so comfortable for years and, to add to her feeling of well-being, she was being paid ten shillings an hour. She was baby-sitting. Her charges were twin girls of nearly four with long, straight hair and fringes. They looked adorable sleeping between their flowered sheets and, although this was her third evening of baby-sitting, she had never seen them awake and didn't much want to. The first evening, she had gone to their bedroom every half-hour to make sure they had not suffocated or fallen out of bed; but now she relaxed and enjoyed herself. The parents had promised her television the next time she came. They were a well-to-do, social young couple who treated her with great consideration, but their manner towards her was remote. At the end of the evening, when the husband drove her home, hardly a word was exchanged.

There was talk of recommending her to their friends and Evelyn was so impressed with her earning capacity that she was buying clothes on credit from a famous store. She had had an account there years ago and, after an assistant had done a little discreet telephoning to the accounts department, it appeared to be still in working order. She had spent two happy mornings re-furbishing her wardrobe and having her hair and hands attended to. She told the assistants she had recently returned from abroad and hadn't a thing to wear, and soon it seemed to her as if it were true and she repeated the same story to a woman she shared a table with in the snack-bar.

When she was asked where she had been living abroad, she said, 'Australia, seven years of it, my dear. One feels so cut off. Mutton for every meal and those boring blue gum trees.'

She felt so affluent she snubbed Harry Rutter when he asked her out to lunch. 'I might be able to manage it, but where do you intend to take me?' she drawled down the telephone. 'Not to that wretched little place you took me to last time. How about the Brompton Grill? It's near and my friends tell me it is excellent.'

They compromised with the Drayton Arms and, as they passed through the bar, Evelyn insisted on a whisky. Her expensive clothes and sleek blue hair intimidated the little man. He thought she must have inherited the money she had been expecting ever since he had known her. When he asked her point-blank, she smiled mysteriously and said, 'I have and I haven't, shall we leave it like that?'

II

'That's new isn't it?' Berti asked, eyeing Evelyn with bitterness. 'Off the peg, obviously. I always had my coats and skirts made for me. It's just a matter of standards and how one had been brought up, I suppose. But whatever induced you to buy black? So aging.'

'If you weren't so blind, you would see that it is charcoal-grey. Every well-dressed woman should have one dark suit in her wardrobe, so useful for informal luncheons and cocktail parties and funerals, of course. By the way, are you going to Jim Clarke's funeral?'

'How can I, in this state? That idiot doctor says I mustn't leave the house for another week. Then I have to go to some wretched hospital and have my arm wrenched about. What a prospect! Do you know, he says I'm curiously allergic to pain. Who isn't?'

'Would you like me to go? After all, I knew the man well enough, although he was your particular friend.'

'Thank you, no,' Berti snapped. 'I don't want you butting in on my affairs.' She re-arranged her headscarf with angry, jerky movements, turning her back on Evelyn, who was slowly walking round the room, posing every now and then in what she hoped was a model-like position.

Berti gazed out of the back window which looked on to the back garden, where Harry Lake's bulbs were already showing. 'Another spring,' she thought sadly. 'Soon the papers will be filled with damn-fool photographs of girls rolling among the daffodils in Hyde Park. Why don't the keepers do their work and shoo the girls away? Breaking down the flowers like that.' She turned to Evelyn who was standing with one hand on her hip and holding an imaginary rope of pearls with the other. She said gruffly, 'On second thoughts, Evelyn, I'd like you to go. I want to know who was there and what sort of funeral they are giving poor old Jim. That son of his will be there, forgotten his name now, but I knew him as a child. His mother left him a fortune when she died; Jim didn't get a thing because they had been separated for years. Yes, you go and if anyone asks who you are, say you're representing me.' She fumbled in her bag and brought out a crumpled obituary notice torn from the *Daily Telegraph*. 'It says here that one has to telephone Allsop, the undertakers, for particulars, so you'd better do it straight away. He has been dead three days already.'

Talking about the coming funeral kept them occupied until it was time for Evelyn to leave for her baby-sitting. She was hoping for television, which she had only seen functioning in shop windows. She had been unsuccessfully trying to induce Amy to buy a set for years.

Jim Clarke was to be buried on the Thursday morning at twelve and Evelyn went off wearing her charcoal-grey coat and skirt and with her head covered with a black mantilla left behind by the Señora. The mantilla was worn with the point facing the back of her head and it was only after Evelyn had left that Berti remembered how the Señora had worn it when she left the house for mass on Sunday mornings. 'Oh, well. Let the woman look the fool she is,' she chuckled to herself as she practised the arm exercises the doctor had advised her to do at frequent intervals. They made not the slightest difference; her arm still remained useless and her hand claw-like. She was unable to re-roll the five cigarettes Amy gave her each day, so she chopped them in half with the carving knife and smoked them to the end in a long jade holder. The thing that really upset her was her hair, long wisps of white with blazing red ends which she kept hidden under a scarf. The fact that she was penniless, and with no prospects, had become too terrible to contemplate.

She was eating her luncheon from a tray when Evelyn returned with a prayer book in one hand and the mantilla in the other. 'You might have told me I was wearing it the wrong way,' she complained. 'A woman at the cemetery pointed it out and I did feel silly. I'll run upstairs and change before I tell you all about it.'

'No. Sit down in that chair by the fire and tell me everything immediately. Was the son there and what was the daughter-in-law like? Jim always referred to her as "that formidable woman".'

'Yes, the son was there. Rather good-looking, dark and taller than his father. His wife has a huge jaw as if she has been chewing gum or iron since birth and she gave me the most horrible looks, thought I was you perhaps; but the lawyer, my dear, he was sweet. I told him I was representing you and he seemed really interested. Wrote down my address too, so I must have made an impression. They all went off to have drinks or lunch afterwards and I could see he was asking the son if I could come along too, but the awful wife put her foot down before he had even finished speaking. The son laughed. Not a nice thing to do at his father's funeral.'

'Were there many there?' Berti asked as she chased a chipped potato round her plate with a fork. 'If I'd been there I'm sure I would have run into lots of old friends I've lost touch with.'

'There were only about six of us there counting me — a sad little funeral, really, and only five wreaths. You should have sent a wreath, Berti.'

'Don't be an idiot. How could I? Anyway, Jim was the last man to care about wilting flowers twisted into circles. He once told me he would like to be buried with a bottle of whisky and a photograph of me. Tell me more. What was she wearing and how did the service go?'

A few days after Jim Clarke was buried Berti received a letter from his solicitor telling her she had been left a legacy of £2,800 in the late James Henry Clarke's will and asking her to call at an office in Bedford Square. At first she thought the letter must be a joke, in very poor taste, but the writing paper appeared real enough and the name, Knibbs, was authentic. She had often heard Jim mention it. Besides acting as his solicitors, they were distantly related; his mother had been a Knibbs.

Trembling with excitement, she rushed to the telephone and, after dialing three wrong numbers, she found herself actually speaking to Mr Knibbs and his reassuring voice answering her questions. He even offered her an advance while the will was going through probate. She made an appointment for the following day. It would be the first time she had left the house since her illness. The letter was shown to Evelyn, who was so overcome with jealousy and excitement that she also had a shaking fit. They went down to the basement together to tell Amy the wonderful news and she was so overwhelmed with relief that she burst into tears. Amy brought out the sherry that was specially kept for her Harry, and Berti's health was drunk, and the three women sat round the kitchen table discussing Berti's good fortune.

Amy suggested timidly, 'An annuity would be best, it really would, Miss Berti. The money will just melt away otherwise.'

Evelyn wildly advised her to 'blow the lot'.

Berti wisely said she would ask Mr Knibbs' advice. 'After all, it's got to last the rest of my life. I'll never get any more. Of course, the first thing I'll do is pay you all I owe, Amy.' She already had the air of a woman of means.

An hour, and three-quarters of a bottle of sherry later Harry Lake came striding into the room and found the three women still sitting at the table, Amy in the process of handing Berti a pound note and saying, 'Are you sure you feel up to going to the hairdresser alone? Perhaps Miss Evelyn had better go with you. Oh, Harry! You did give me a start!'

Harry scowled. 'Got nothing better to do with your morning than to sit drinking?' he said heavily. 'I had some news for you, but it can wait.' He turned away, as if to leave.

Amy cried, 'Don't go, dear. We are only celebrating. Miss Berti's come into money, thousands of pounds. Show him the letter, Miss Berti.' Berti leapt up and, flinging her good arm round the disconcerted police-man, entreated him to drink her health. Evelyn pushed a glass of sherry into his hand. Disengaging himself, he sipped it with an air of disapproval; although he did say, 'Your health, Miss,' fixing a cold blue eye on Berti.

Chattering wildly, she backed towards the door: 'The poor man, I wouldn't have had him die for the world, even if his hearing aid was broken and he couldn't hear a thing. But it's wonderful, isn't it, when you think I only had one-and-fourpence in my bag this morning? I do assure you, I'll pay Amy all I owe. Well, I'm off to have my hair done.' She patted her headscarf which had slipped forward and almost covered her eyes, gave a nervous little wave of the hand and backed through the door, followed by Evelyn

Amy said, 'I'm sorry, dear. It was such wonderful news, we had to have a little celebration. Now, what was it you had to tell me?' She cleared the table of the offending bottle and glasses and wiped it over with a cloth.

'It's about Hetty,' Harry said gravely. 'You asked me to see what she was up to and, this morning being a Thursday, my day off, I followed her.'

'Oh!' Amy gazed at Harry, 'yes, you followed her?'

'And I found her with a man.' The sherry was taking effect and Harry was beginning to enjoy himself.

'A man!' Amy gasped.

'Yes, one of those two-legged things that wear trousers and shave.'

'Don't make a joke of it, Harry. For heaven's sake, tell me what she was doing with this man!'

'She was kneeling in a lonely, wild garden with him. I crept into an old summer-house filled with cats and they never noticed me.'

'They were praying, then, in this garden? What a strange thing to do. What sort of a man was he? A clergyman?'

'Hardly. A gentleman perhaps, but certainly not a clergyman. I'd say he was a bit cracked, but harmless. Wears a huge pair of gloves hanging from his neck on a tape.'

'I can't understand it.' Amy wrinkled her smooth forehead and sighed. 'Hetty kneeling with a man not quite right in the head. Are you sure they were praying? They could have been weeding.'

'That's just like a woman. I never said they were praying, I said kneeling. Actually, they were making pictures out of bits of china and stone, very good they were too.'

'What did they say when they saw you?'

'They didn't see me. I passed quite close but they were so absorbed they never looked up. I don't think there's much to worry about, as long as she doesn't miss school. Tell her she can only go on Saturdays and see what happens.'

'Yes, I suppose you're right, you usually are. But it all seems very queer to me,' Amy said dejectedly.

Harry lightly touched her face with his fingers. 'Don't worry, old girl. I'm sorry I was a bit annoyed when I came in. I didn't like seeing you drinking with those crazy old women, all bent over the table like witches, and you handing out pound notes. Now, what about coming to the pictures this afternoon? We could take Hetty if you like. Give her a bit of a talking to, then the film as a sweetener.'

When Hetty came home she found Harry Lake, wearing one of her mother's aprons, frying chips while her mother beat up eggs for an omelette.

She stood by the door, waiting for her mother's outburst and muttered, 'I'm sorry, Mummy, I haven't been to school again. I had to come home because I was starving.'

She survived the little talk with only a few tears to show for it and they were really shed because Glover and the garden were no longer secret and the mosaics had been seen by other eyes. With the tears still wet upon her cheeks she asked her mother if she could bring a kitten home, a pure white tom called Prince. Amy exchanged glances with Harry. He nodded his head and the kitten was reluctantly agreed to on the condition that she only went to the garden on Saturdays.

So Hetty played truant no more and Prince Vronsky became a member of Amy Doll's household and had kittens regularly, twice a year.

Evelyn accompanied Berti to Mr Knibbs' office. The interview was most satisfactory, both women dressed in mournful clothes and behaving with great decorum. Berti was handed a cheque for £100 for immediate necessities and advised to buy an annuity with at least £2,500 of the legacy.

She agreed when, to her surprise, she discovered that for once her age was an asset. 'And the longer I last, the more annoyed they'll be,' she laughed. 'What an incentive to live to a great age!' Then, remembering her almost widowed state, added, 'But I don't think I could stand the loneliness.'

When they left the office the solicitor turned to his clerk and said, 'Those gallant old ladies, one has lost the use of her arm, and her brother, a general, died recently and left her totally unprovided for and the other is reduced to baby-sitting. They are too proud to apply for State help, so we must do all we can to help them.'

Actually, that evening, Evelyn's career as a baby-sitter came abruptly to an end. She had been recommended by the mother of the twin girls to a young couple who lived in Chelsea. This time she was to mind an eight-month-old boy, blissfully asleep with his thumb in his mouth.

'He usually sleeps for hours,' the young mother explained. 'But if he does wake up, there's a bottle all prepared; hold it under the hot tap for a few minutes to take the chill off and he'll wolf it down. He's recovering from a cold, so keep an eye on him to make sure he doesn't get uncovered, but it's unlikely he'll move, he's such a heavy sleeper.' She called to her husband, 'I'll be ready in a moment, darling. Must do my nails.'

Evelyn went into the drawing-room, where a meal was prepared for her under a napkin. The husband was standing with his back to the fire with a dry martini in his hand.

He bowed to Evelyn and said, 'Thank God you've come. Our last baby-sitter let us down and we haven't been out for a month.' She eyed his glass with longing. 'Would you care for a martini to carry you through a lonely evening?' he asked. Evelyn accepted the drink coyly, saying she wasn't used to it and hoped it wouldn't make her drunk. Then the wife came in, holding out her drying finger-nails. She raised her rather aggressive eyebrows when she saw Evelyn and her husband drinking together, refused a drink herself, gave Evelyn a few last-minute instructions and bustled her husband out of the house.

Evelyn was left in charge. The first thing she did was

to lift up the napkin and examine the meal that had been left for her – cold chicken with salad and a lemon mousse. Adequate, but slightly dull. Then she explored the little house, which was furnished in an interesting jumble of antique and modern. The dining-room had dark blue walls and white furniture, the bedroom had a draped canopy over the double bed, held in place by a battered cupid with an arm missing. 'Berti,' she said and giggled. She admired herself in front of the large oval looking-glass. Not bad, she thought, for sixty-two; and she sniffed the various bottles of scent on the dressing-table and dabbed a little Madame Rochas behind her ears. She peered in the wardrobes, then, feeling guilty, scuttled into the kitchen. It was surprisingly untidy, with baby's napkins slung across the ceiling, but filled with electric appliances. The refrigerator was scarlet and the washing machine enormous and studded with knobs, but what fascinated her most was the dish-washing machine. She stood in front of it, longing to put it into motion, but decided against this and returned to the drawing-room. She looked round for a television set, but there was only a small white radio – she had been looking forward to the next installment of 'The Avengers'. Disappointed, she searched in the magazine rack, only to find it stuffed with architectural and art papers, but the bookcase proved a little better and she helped herself to a Colette.

Before she settled down to her meal she examined the baby, who was still sleeping although he had managed to get uncovered. As she gingerly tucked him under the blankets, the blue eyes opened for an awful moment, then closed, and the thumb went back into his mouth. She noticed a clean napkin on a chair by the cot, obviously a hint to change the child if anything drastic happened. In a panic she rushed back to the sitting-room. The fact that the child might expect to have its napkin changed had never entered her head and she remembered hearing stories about unskilled baby-minders piercing the baby's stomach, or even worse, with pins.

She seated herself at the table and started her cold supper and, as she ate, her eyes wandered round the room and lighted on the gin and vermouth standing invitingly on a small side-table. Her empty glass was beside her and she thought, 'They will never know if I just have another half-glass to steady my nerves.' When she poured the gin out she almost filled the glass by mistake, but there was nothing she could do except drink it, now the vermouth had mixed with the gin. Her meal finished, she went to look at the sleeping baby. It was uncovered again and making little sounds. There were at least two hours to go before the parents were due to return and the baby seemed alarmingly restless. 'I won't go near it unless it screams, but what can I do if it does scream?' she thought miserably. She returned to the drawing-room and picked up the Colette. It was an untranslated edition. She struggled with the French but found she was extraordinarily sleepy and her head was nodding over the book. 'It would be terrible if they found me asleep,' she thought. 'What I really need is another drink to stimulate me.'

She left her chair and unsteadily made her way toward the bottles. She scrutinized them for a few minutes. There appeared to be quite a lot of gin, but the vermouth was low. So she decided to have a small neat gin. Her hands weren't very steady and she spilt some on the table and made futile little dabs with her handkerchief to mop it up. Her glass was almost full and the gin had gone down considerably. There was a bowl which had contained ice-cubes which had now turned to water, so she tipped a little water into her glass and, on second thoughts, poured the rest into the gin bottle. She had a certain amount of trouble fixing the cap, mopped up the table again and sat down with her almost-neat gin. She found her French was coming back nicely although the top of her head was throbbing for some strange reason. She sat swaying as she read aloud, slower and slower until she fell asleep.

When she awoke she had no idea where she was; it seemed as if she was in some horrible dream. An angry woman was shouting at her, a baby was yelling at the top of its lungs and an unknown young man was shaking her by the shoulder. She staggered to her feet and asked, 'What's all the noise about? Is there a fire or something?'

The angry young woman was standing in the doorway with the still-screaming baby in her arms. 'How dare you call yourself a baby-sitter?' she demanded. 'The poor little thing is frozen and must have been crying for hours and his nappy's dirty. It's your fault if he gets pneumonia and dies.'

Evelyn stood swaying and caught on to the back of the chair for support. 'Oh dear, I must have dozed off for a few minutes, so sorry. I don't seem to be feeling very well.' She looked at her accusers with unfocussed eyes and mumbled, 'Better go home, you know, very tired.'

'John,' the baby's mother screamed hysterically, 'the woman's drunk! Our baby has been left in the charge of a drunkard who might have dropped him or burnt him to death. Oh, God! It was your fault for giving her a drink in the first place. Get her out of the house immediately or I'll call the police.' She bounced off, clutching her yelling child.

'Yes, I'll take her home immediately,' the husband agreed eagerly. 'Come, Miss . . . Miss whatever you're called. I'll drive you home if you tell me where you live. Not here, in the car.' He took her by the arm, steered her out of the house and roughly pushed her into the back seat of the car. He settled himself in the driving seat, muttering, 'Oh, Lord, oh, Lord!' as he searched for the ignition key. He turned round to Evelyn. 'Tell me where the hell you live and if you're sick in the car, I'll murder you,' he snarled.

'Oh, Oh, I do feel so ill, must be food poisoning,' she moaned. 'So kind of you to give me a lift.' She gave her address and collapsed in the seat with her handkerchief held over her mouth. When they reached Mulberry Grove he propelled her up the steps and, taking her handbag, extracted the key, and let her into the house. He did not drive away immediately, but sat smoking in the car, waiting for things to quieten at home.

12

After a night of sickness, Evelyn sat holding a cup of black coffee between her shaking hands. On the table before her lay a bill for fifty-seven pounds, six shillings and ninepence. 'It must be some mistake,' she wailed to Amy. 'I couldn't have spent all that. I know for a fact that I never bought anything costing ninepence. Here, take the blasted bill and check it for me. I feel an absolute wreck this morning – food poisoning. Those people I went to last night gave me poisoned chicken so I shan't be going there again. Remember, if they 'phone.'

Amy draped her duster over the broom handle and gingerly took the piece of paper Evelyn held out. Bills and debts were terrible words to her. She carefully studied each item with its date. 'The six-and-ninepence was for hosiery, Miss Evelyn, and that coat and skirt you had, the dark one, cost twenty-two guineas, and here's a twin-set for ten, and then you bought those skin-tight, violet-coloured trousers and green ditto and the silk shirt. I can't make it all out but you seem to have been extremely extravagant. Didn't you ask about the prices when you bought the things?'

Evelyn smiled wanly. 'I wasn't brought up to ask how

much things cost; we ordered the best, whatever the price. I remember as a child running round my father's palace dressed in pure silk from head to foot. It's difficult to change my habits at my age, so they will just have to wait for their money. Anyway, I'm sure the ninepence is an overcharge. Hell! Now the coffee's gone cold.'

The door opened and Berti peered round the door. Her hair, at last free from the headscarf, was now dyed a softer shade of red. The face below had aged considerably; but she still had her beautiful profile and, conscious of this, she had formed a new habit of turning away from whoever she was speaking to and talking over her shoulder.

'Well, dears,' she called cheerfully, 'would either of you like to come with me to the hospital? I'm off for my hour of torture.'

Evelyn shook her head. 'Can't you see I'm not well? I've been poisoned.'

'Really? I thought I heard someone being sick during the night and the lavatory stinks of gin. You didn't have a go at the baby's bottle, by any chance?' Berti turned to Amy, who was making for the door with her cleaning things. 'Won't you come with me, Amy? It's so depressing alone, with them all hobbling about on sticks, grumbling and groaning.'

'No, miss,' Amy said, with only her head appearing through the door. 'Harry's coming to start on the wall-papering upstairs. He's turning what used to be the Señora's room into a swinging room for Hetty, three walls pink and one navy blue. He's dying to get his hands on this room. You *are* looking for other accommodation, aren't you?' The head disappeared and the door was firmly shut.

'She's scared stiff we won't go,' Berti laughed ruefully.

Evelyn held her head and moaned, 'She can't really turn us out, can she?'

'She certainly can. Policeman Harry hates the sight of us. He wrecked our little business and now he's turning us out into the streets. Extraordinary, a great girl of that age swinging – and in her bedroom, too. Well, I'm off.'

Left to herself, Evelyn finished her cold coffee and pushed the offending invoice under yesterday's *Daily Telegraph*. As she did so, the name Hunter caught her eye – Hunter without Smith, still it could be a relation. It was a death notice for Claude Harold Hunter, dearly loved husband of Grace, who was to be cremated at Golders Green on Friday at three o'clock and wanted sprays only, by request. 'Even if I'm feeling poorly, I think I ought to go. I'm sure I remember Mother mentioning Sir Claude. He could easily be a relation,' she persuaded herself as she turned hopefully to the obituaries. But Sir Claude was not mentioned. With the newspaper under her arm she went up to the room, took an aspirin and laid her funeral clothes on the bed. She wished she had a little black hat, a velvet turban perhaps. Still, the mantilla was rather romantic. She might even be mistaken for the widow, Lady Hunter.

When Berti returned from the hospital she found Evelyn dressed in her charcoal grey, spooning up tinned tomato soup.

'I'm just off to my cousin's funeral,' she cried excitedly. 'Sir Claude Hunter, you must have heard me mention him and his wife, Grace. She telephoned after you left.'

For once, Berti was speechless and it was a few minutes before she could bring out, 'Strange they never asked you to visit them or sent a card at Christmas.' Evelyn was still explaining how it had happened that she had lost touch with her cousins when Berti left the room with a purposeful expression on her face. She took a tin of sardines from the kitchen and went down to Amy to ask her to open it. As Amy was turning the key of the tin, she asked casually, 'By the way, were there any telephone calls while I was out?'

'Sorry, I can't get the tin completely open, the key's that stiff,' Amy said as she handed her the half-open tin. 'Telephone calls? No, of course not. Didn't you know, the 'phone's out of order? Harry damaged the wires with his painting. I expect they'll be along tomorrow to see to the repairs; but we can't count on it.'

Berti rushed upstairs, spilling oil as she went, but Evelyn had left for Golders Green and wouldn't return for hours.

The funeral turned out to be even better than Evelyn had hoped. After giving her name as Hunter she was accepted as a member of the family and drove away from the cemetery in one of the funeral cars. When questioned by a fellow passenger, an old lady wearing a wig and false eyelashes, she told her that she had been living abroad for years and had hardly seen her cousin Claude since his marriage to Grace. 'But I remember her wedding, she was such a lovely bride.'

The sunken eyes behind the false eyelashes came alive and burned at Evelyn.

'Strange,' she said, giving a spiteful little laugh, 'strange that you should have been at the wedding. They were married in India.'

Evelyn smiled and said without hesitation, 'Yes, it was a coincidence that I happened to be there at that particular time. I was staying with Colonel Pilkington, my mother's half-brother; you may have met him, he was an absolute charmer.'

'No. I've never met anyone called Pilkington. It was Pilkington you said? Oh, here we are. I see the blinds aren't drawn; just like Grace, no respect for the dead.'

A grey-faced man, nursing his hat on his knees, suddenly vibrated with indignation: 'Yes, indeed, rushing the poor man into his grave when he's only been dead three days.'

The car had drawn up outside a cream-painted early Victorian house. Evelyn had no idea where they were, but, as she looked round for landmarks, she heard another guest say something about Lord's cricket ground and gathered that they might possibly be in St John's Wood. There were over twenty people streaming into the house and Evelyn turned away from her travelling companions and kept close to a heavy, stupid-looking woman accompanied by a daughter as heavy and stupid-looking as her mother. She felt she could cope with them if they started asking questions.

Tea was served in the drawing-room by a white-coated man-servant and the guests stood about in little groups, balancing their cups of tea and chattering as if it were a garden party. No one appeared to be mourning Sir Claude.

His widow, supported by her two tall sons, mingled with her guests, saying from time to time, 'How good of you to come! I hope you are being looked after.' She battered her eyes at Evelyn and said, 'How sweet of you to come! I haven't seen you for ages.' Evelyn said she had been living abroad for years and had only recently returned. 'Yes, yes. Of course, I remember.' Lady Hunter smiled and went on to the heavy mother and daughter. Later Evelyn heard her remark to one of her sons, 'I can't quite place that tall thin woman who is enjoying her tea so much.'

The son replied, 'She's called Hunter — a second cousin of Daddy's. Been abroad for years, but remembers me as a baby.'

Lady Hunter narrowed her eyes. 'So she says,' she said cryptically. Evelyn felt it was time she left.

As soon as she entered the house in Mulberry Grove she was pounced on by Berti. 'So you were telephoned this morning by your cousin Hunter and the damn thing's been out of order since yesterday,' she crowed.

Evelyn was tired. She was over-filled with cake and her shoes were hurting her feet. The sight of Berti's raddled face sickened her. 'Damn and blast you, you nosey old hag,' she shouted. 'If you want to know, I saw the announcement and went out and telephoned Grace myself, so put that in your pipe and smoke it. I've had a lovely afternoon, a drive in a huge car and tea at my cousin's house, where I met lots of old friends and relations and thoroughly enjoyed myself.' She pushed past Berti and marched upstairs on her aching feet. Berti stood in the hall, her jaw trembling with unspoken words.

A few days later the newspapers announced the death of a famous actress. After reading, and remarking on, the account of her successful life, Berti munched her breakfast toast thoughtfully. 'You've made it bloody hard this morning,' she said quite affably to Evelyn who had received her quarterly cheque for £75 and was doing sums on the back of the envelope.

'Really?' Evelyn said, frowning at her figures. 'Splendid for the teeth if it doesn't break them. I think I'll pay Amy weekly in future. No good paying her a month in advance when she intends to chuck us out at her own convenience.'

'Perhaps you are right. Do you think it would be a good idea if we went to Mary North's funeral tomorrow? We'd see a lot of celebrities and it'd only cost us the fare to Highgate.'

'Excellent idea.' Evelyn pushed the cheque and figures into her pocket. 'There's something about a funeral, as long as it isn't your own, of course. I must say, I enjoyed the two I've been to recently. Did I ever tell you about my father's funeral and how the villagers fought for the honour of carrying the coffin over the stony, snowy ground. The squire meant a lot to them in those days.'

'Only too true.' Berti's eyes became dreamy with invention. 'I remember our butler, er, old Leathers, standing in the hall with tears running down his cheeks the day my father died. The men pulled him all the way to the church, in one of the estate wagons, I mean. It was heaped with wreaths and little nosegays from the village children . . .' Her voice trailed away as she tried to remember what had actually happened when her father died. She knew it had occurred shortly after she had left school but couldn't recall a thing about it. It must have happened when she was staying with that boring family in Dresden, supposed to be learning German. If she remembered rightly, she had only been there a few weeks before she was recalled home and afterwards they had moved to that horrible little house near Stevenage. Yes, that was how it had been. Her father had died while she was in Germany and they hadn't been left as well off as they expected. There had even been talk of her being sent off somewhere as a governess; but she soon escaped to London on the pretext of learning shorthand and typing and life had rushed to meet her.

Both women sat over the breakfast table dreaming of the past, real and imagined, until the telephone, which had recovered from Harry's painting, shrilled. There was no longer the competition to answer it that there used to be and they slowly stirred themselves and exchanged glances before Berti decided the call might be for her and rose to answer it. When she left the table, Evelyn took out her envelope and studied her figures again in the hope of making her £75 last for the next three months. She had decided it was impossible, even if she only paid half her debts, when Berti bustled towards her with a triumphant expression on her face.

'Marvellous news! I've got us a flat, at least, Knibbs has found it. I called in the other day and told him our difficulties, how we were being turned out and so on, and now the dear man has produced this wonderful flat for only three pounds a week. It's in Highgate, in the basement of a doctor's house and we have to answer the telephone for a few hours each evening, that's why it is so cheap. Oh, and there's an Aga like Amy's, for heating the water, that has to be made up twice a day. The char brings the buckets in; but we have to do the actual stoking, at least, you'd have to; that is, if you would like to share the flat. Electricity and hot water are all included, so our expenses would be almost nil. Anyway, I'm seeing it tomorrow. I'd better dress in a restrained manner, don't you think?' Breathlessly, she darted from the room to tell Amy the news.

Evelyn still sat at the breakfast table, biting a thumbnail thoughtfully. Then she folded the envelope containing her figures and slipped it back in her pocket. Reluctantly, she decided to accept Berti's offer.

13

In Highgate the following evening, when the last patient had left the surgery, the doctor's wife unbuttoned her white overall and said, 'Good news, dear. I've let the flat to the two elderly ladies Knibbs recommended. They're older than I expected and one has a withered arm, but the younger one assured me she could manage the boiler, said there was a similar one where they are now. They both appeared to be in mourning, the tall one's brother had just died. A general, she said, and it may be true. And she said something about having to give up an exclusive little business, a boutique, I suppose. They have an air of breeding; but there is something distinctly odd about them, I couldn't quite put my finger on it. Still, at least they can't produce an illegitimate baby like the last woman we had – and there was the deaf one. They both seemed to hear perfectly and used to the telephone. They have charming voices. It's just their oddness that makes me a little nervous. Oh, yes, and they'd been to a funeral at the cemetery and I heard the one with blue hair whisper to the other, "Handy for funerals, isn't it?" Perhaps they're body-snatchers.'

* * *

Amy and Harry walked in the Mulberry Grove garden admiring the tulips that were just about to flower among the forget-me-nots.

'The whole three dozen have come up and not a dud amongst them. Can you smell the wallflowers, love?'

Amy sniffed and smelt haddock simmering in milk coming through the kitchen window. 'Yes, they smell a treat,' she said, taking Harry's arm. 'They've gone to see this flat I was telling you about, and, if all goes well, they'll be out of the house in a week, or fortnight at the most, and we'll have the place to ourselves, except for Hetty, of course.' She glanced at Harry shyly.

'Shall we make it Whitsun, then? We could spend a few days with my family, you know, for our honey-moon, unless you'd rather go somewhere else, but I do want you to meet my mother and the rest of them. I suppose Hetty will have to come along too,' he added rather sadly. Step-daughters were all very well, but he didn't want to take one on his honeymoon. Such a big girl, too, towering over her mother.

Amy laughed self-consciously. 'No, no, of course not. She could stay with my friend, Doris, or perhaps someone from the school would have her for a week. For all they're so grand, she's got friends there. Don't worry.'

'I'm not worrying,' Harry said stolidly. 'I'll see about the licence, then. We'll make it the Friday, shall we, dear?' They kissed in the gathering dusk while the haddock dried in the oven.

As Hetty munched her breakfast cornflakes her mother jerked out her marriage plans. 'And then, you see, Harry wants me to meet his family. Well, they live in Leamington. We may be away a few days or even a week, so I'll have to make some arrangements about

you: I think we had better go on our own the first time,
you do understand, Hetty?'

'Yes, of course I understand; you don't want me on
your honeymoon. Couldn't I stay with Doris and Solly?'

Amy frowned. 'I've thought about that, but don't
consider it suitable. Such a damp little house, almost a
slum really, and Doris doesn't talk very nice. Couldn't
one of your school-friends put you up? It's only for a
week.'

'I'll put it round. Jenny's family have a huge house in
Holland Park. She knows you're getting married, they
all do.'

'How can they? I've only just told you,' Amy snapped
as she left the table and bustled towards the scullery,
where bacon fried.

'Oh, Mother. Don't be so silly. I've known it for
months. We're all thrilled about it. By the way, I'll have
to take Vronsky, I mean Prince, with me.'

Amy banged a plate of bacon and eggs in front of her
daughter. 'That cat's been making messes among Harry's wallflowers and he's so proud of their scent.'

'It's better than using my wellington boots; I'll never
be able to wear them again.'

Hetty decided that, in spite of being bribed with a
swinging bedroom and a kitten, she'd have to skip
school that morning in the hope of meeting Glover. She
had the idea that it might be amusing to stay with his
family while her mother was away. Glover talked about
them endlessly and she had become fascinated by them.
His mother so old and frail, with great hollows behind
her eyes, grew miniature trees in pots and, on her good
days, played the harp. Sister Agnes painted water col-
ours at a golden easel and owned a canary who laid

eggs which never hatched: 'She always takes him from the room when we eat chicken, of course.' The house appeared to be filled with treasures; a musical box, all inlaid with mother-of-pearl, which played six different tunes: fans made of coloured feathers: a picture which changed from a ship to a lion – it depended from which angle you looked at it. There was a swing in the garden and, in Glover's bedroom, a rowing machine, bought to strengthen him when he was young. 'I rowed and rowed, but never got anywhere, I've given it up now.'

She left the bus and, dodging a few school hats, made for their deserted garden. Their latest mosaic – they were working on it together – was a Noah's ark with the dove flying above. The dove and the ark were white, they were seldom short of white china, but the roof of the ark was multi-coloured and a considerable amount of china from Glover's house had been sacrificed. Among other things he had managed to smuggle out a huge green and gold soup tureen and some bronze and blue Crown Derby plates. 'There's a whole china pantry crammed with the stuff, they'll never miss it,' he said cheerfully as he hammered the china into handy pieces with a stone.

She saw Glover standing disconsolately outside the house, gloveless and muttering to himself. There was the sound of men hammering and shouting and a great clanking going on. The 'For Sale' notices had a red 'Sold' painted on them now and there were builder's boards displayed. Kitely Bros, Builders and Constructors, had taken over.

Glover tottered towards Hetty, flapping his huge hands. 'Don't go in, it's heartbreaking,' he cried brokenly. 'Bags of cement and sand all over the place, iron scaffolding too, long tubes of it, and our mosaics are trampled on – what's left of them, that is. Vandalism, that's all it is. And there's a man like a gorilla making tea in the summer-house.'

'But we'd almost finished. How ghastly!' She took a small yellow saucer from her school satchel. 'Look, the dove's beak; you remember, we decided on yellow.' She flung the saucer into the road and watched a passing taxi crunch it to smithereens.

Glover said, 'It isn't only this vandalism. My mother's ill, Hester, and if anything happened to her it would be terrible, terrible. I wouldn't know what to do. Clothes would be such a problem, to know when to change them and that sort of thing and when to cast wool on and off. Then there would be meals to be ordered. And there's money. Cheques to sign and goodness knows what. How would I know when to pay the rates and order coal?'

'But your sister, Agnes, couldn't she look after that sort of thing?'

'I suppose so; but I'm the eldest. I'd be the head of the house. There's a nurse there now, a very nice woman. She sent me out for a bit, said she'd make me some cocoa at half-past-eleven, but if anything happened to Mother, she'd go away and I'd be alone with Agnes. She's all right, but she's impatient and quite snappy at times, speaks to me as if I were dotty, or something. She was disappointed over a young school-master and it has soured her, Mother says.' He looked at his cowboy watch. 'Eleven-fifteen already. I'd better get back. The nurse will be waiting, mustn't disappoint her.' He ambled off without saying goodbye and Hetty knew they would never see each other again. She decided to go to school after all and make some excuse about being late.

* * *

Berti and Evelyn were packing. Packing and running up and down stairs, calling to each other, swearing and bothering Amy. 'Have you a large cardboard box, Amy? String? Wrapping paper? Would Hetty like this manicure set? Half of it is missing, but it might come in useful. This hairbrush? Most of the bristles have gone, but it's real silver — look at the hall-mark. How about these gloves, seven of them, all odd but handmade, beautiful quality. Perhaps you could match or dye them. Are all the coat-hangers in the cupboard yours or mine? Amy, can you unlock this case for me, so difficult with only one hand. Oh, it's rusted, has it? Would you bring some oil?'

Then Evelyn had to be instructed on how to work the Aga, which resulted in it going out several times so that Amy had the trouble of raking it out and re-lighting. Berti and Evelyn visited the basement separately to discuss the difficulties of their future life together.

'She'll try to make a slave of me because I have two hands,' Evelyn complained tearfully. 'I'll be the one to clean and wash up and do all the donkey work. She says she will do the shopping and that means we'll only eat what she likes — and it will be the same with television. Did you know she's buying a set? But will I ever be allowed to see a programme I want? She can't bear to see pretty girls now she's such a fright herself, so I suppose we'll only have to look at men.'

Then Berti came down and complained, 'To think I'll have to end my days with that idiot. She tells the most unconvincing lies about her family background. A pity, really, if we both spoke the truth, we'd have quite a new line of conversation. I've paid her debts for her, and, if she runs up any more, I'll kick her out. I'm not having Harry Rutter there either, wretched little man.

And there's going to be trouble over the wardrobe. There's only one and that's in my room and I'm damned if I'm going to share it. She'll have to hang her clothes behind the curtain in the hall. One good thing, we've arranged that I'm to do the shopping. If it was left to her she'd be bringing home baskets filled with smoked salmon and strawberries, all on credit as likely as not.'

Amy was worn out with them. Yet, when the day of departure at last came, she was almost reluctant to part with her tiresome lodgers. They had been part of her life for so long and, although she was so much younger, she felt almost motherly towards them. They had bought her a parting present of magnificent pink nylon sheets with pillow cases to match.

'Double sheets, of course,' Berti laughed as she hugged Amy with one stick-like arm. There was an enormous box of chocolates for Hetty, all decked with violets and ribbons.

When the taxi driver saw all their luggage piled outside the house he said they needed a 'bloody pantechnicon' and refused to take the three carved mirrors and the little gilt tables.

'We can't leave them behind,' Evelyn pleaded, 'they have such happy memories for us.'

Berti screeched, 'Happy memories, my foot! They're our props and we may well need them. Look, cabby, I'll give you double fare to Highgate if you'll squeeze them in somehow.'

Eventually the overloaded taxi drove away, with Berti and Evelyn both crying, perched on the pull-down seat and facing a mound of luggage. A heated argument appeared to be going on and Amy had a fleeting glimpse of Berti slapping Evelyn's face. The taxi seemed to be vibrating.

That evening, when Amy was wandering round the empty rooms of her house planning improvements, a shaking Evelyn arrived on the doorstep clutching a split paper carrier bag and a suitcase. 'The rest will have to come by Carter Paterson. I've come back, Amy. I can't share a flat with that fiend of a woman. She wants the entire wardrobe and expects me to hang my clothes behind a curtain like a servant.'

Amy sighed and said, 'Come downstairs and have a cup of tea while we think what to do for the best. I'll tell you what, you can have my wardrobe, the mahogany one that was my mother's. There's a built-in one in our new room, so we won't miss it. I'll send it on tomorrow. While you're drinking your tea I'll 'phone Miss Berti and tell her what we have arranged. But you certainly can't stay here because Harry's got the day off tomorrow and he's coming to attack your room first thing. I've stripped the bed and it's all prepared. Wallpaper with stripes on one wall and plastic paint on the others, I think that's what Harry's planned. He has some strange ideas.'

It was over an hour before Evelyn reluctantly left, dragging her case as if it were filled with lead. Amy watched her out of sight. She wondered what Harry would say about her giving away a perfectly good wardrobe intended for the basement flat they planned to let furnished to a young policeman and his wife.

On the Friday before Whitsun Amy and Harry were married at a church in the nearby Boltons with black angels round the spire. Harry's brother and his wife acted as witnesses and Hetty was a self-appointed bridesmaid. After the ceremony and a substantial luncheon at the Drayton Arms, the bride and groom drove off in a second-hand car Harry had bought for the honeymoon; Amy sitting forward with her eyes fixed on the speedometer, squeaking nervously every time the needle registered more than forty. She was afraid that if the wheels went too fast, they would spin off.

One morning, soon after they returned from their honeymoon, Amy looked up from the basement window and recognized Doris's stout legs pacing the front garden. She opened the back door and called to her and Doris thundered down the steps.

'I didn't know if you'd be up or down,' she gasped, then clapped her hand to her mouth and said archly, 'is the coast clear? I don't want to disturb you if Harry's here.'

'No, Harry's at the station, won't be home for hours,' Amy said coldly. 'Now you're here, come in and have a coffee.' She led the way into the old kitchen.

Doris eyed the partly dismantled basement. 'So you've got rid of those old bells you were always going on about – and the dresser?'

Amy nodded. 'Yes, I was sorry to see it go, but Harry's modernizing the place for a young policeman who is getting married. They seem a nice young couple and are paying five-pounds-ten a week, furnished, of course.' She lit the gas stove.

Doris sat down and, leaning forward in her chair, her hands locked together in her lap and her eyes bright with excitement, asked, 'Well how did it go? Did you enjoy yourself and wasn't it lovely being in bed with a man again after all these years?'

Amy spooned brown powder into the cups. 'It's only instant, I'm afraid,' she said without looking up. 'I wish you wouldn't talk like that, Doris. You make things seem dirty. We had a wonderful honeymoon and that's all I'm saying.'

'What's the family like? You don't mind me asking about them, do you?'

'No, of course not. They were lovely people, Doris, particularly Harry's mother. Ever so cheerful and artistic with it. Designs embroidery, and she's painted swallows flying round the walls of the porch and, would you believe it, butterflies on the door of the outside convenience. There's one indoors as well.'

'What sort of a place is Leamington?' Doris asked as she helped herself to extra sugar, 'lively?'

'No, you couldn't call it lively; sort of dignified and very clean. There's beautiful country around and we went over Shakespeare's house, Warwick Castle and another one beginning with a K, I can't remember its name. It made such a difference having the car and Harry's a superb driver when he doesn't drive too fast. You shouldn't take all that sugar, dear, you're over-weight as it is.'

'I know. It isn't only eating, it's laughing that makes me grow fat. You remember. I've always been one for laughing and the things those men say when I'm serving them; but I don't suppose you want to hear.'

'No, I don't.' Amy changed the subject and said brightly, 'We should be moving upstairs in just over a week. There's only the new kitchen to be finished.'

'Which room will you sleep in, then?'

'The one I had before, you know, when Alf was here. The front one over the drawing-room.'

Doris smiled, 'Miss Berti's room! I suppose you've changed it, but think what must have gone on there. Give Harry a bit of inspiration, eh?'

'Now, Doris, I don't want that kind of talk. Did I tell

you Harry's family are giving us a television set for a wedding present? All clubbing together, you know. I'm really looking forward to it because the wireless doesn't seem the same now since Mrs Dale lost her Diary. It is just Mrs Dale now.'

Doris drained her cup and bent down to pull up her stockings, a sign she was about to leave. 'Tell me how they went off, the old ladies – if you can call them ladies, poor old things. I haven't seen you since they left,' she asked as she adjusted her suspenders.

'Oh, I forgot to tell you, I went to see them as soon as I returned. They weighed on my mind somehow, but I needn't have worried. They've settled down very well, considering. They have got a television which gives them something to quarrel about and are managing with Miss Evelyn's allowance and this annuity Miss Berti has bought. That old man leaving her his money was a God-send. They could have had help from the N.A.B., it's changed its name now, but they swore at me when I suggested it. It's all turned out for the best, though. They've taken up such an unusual hobby, doesn't cost them a penny. They read those death notices in the newspapers and pick on the funerals they'd like to see and go to them like other people go to the cinema. Sometimes they manage to get in the cars and have refreshments and all that. Strange, isn't it?'

'And when they die, I wonder who will go to their funerals.'

'They can go to each other's,' Amy said comfortably.

Doris fumbled in her handbag and brought out her powder-compact. 'Well, it's an improvement on their last hobby, anyway. I'd better be off now. Solly will be home for his dinner today as it's my day off. You know, I'll miss this place. It won't be the same with all these policeman all over the house, more like an effing police station. I suppose I'll have to blow a whistle instead of ringing the bell. Still, you are happy and that is the main thing, dear. Here's a little present for you; open it when I'm gone.' She laid a small package on the table and heaved herself from her chair.

When Doris had gone, Amy stood by the table with the unopened package in her hand. Was the house getting like an effing police station? She wondered. Still, it was a comfort to be on the right side of the law.

CANDIDA CREWE

Accommodating Molly

Molly Almond and Nick Winter make a wonderfully compatible working duo. Practical and attractive, Molly assists in the shop that is Winter Books, dressing the window and charming the customers.

She also listens patiently and attentively to the daily particulars that make Nick's life such a magnificent shambles. Rejecting at least two of the women who love him, Nick himself comes to experience the loss of something never gained: the bafflement and wretchedness of unrequited love.

But Molly is also a victim of unreciprocated feelings. And with her quirky, fatalistic eye, only she knows if she is better equipped to contend with the fickle promises of men.

Candida Crewe takes a wry, sly and knowing look at the age-old battle between the sexes, and finds it just as cruel among the quiet shelves of a London bookshop.

'Bang up-to-date and slyly accurate in its observation of a certain kind of sub-literary life in London.' *Guardian*

PATRICE CHAPLIN

Forget Me Not

It began with the glimpse of a man. When Vicky caught sight of Serge Marais on television, she felt that she had encountered her romantic destiny. Here was the kind of lover of which fantasies are made — an internationally-celebrated conductor, charismatic and handsome, a man to whom the world paid homage. Vicky pursued him, not knowing he was destined to love her.

Fantasies should never come true. For a while there was too much joy, too much passion. Serge was prepared to sacrifice his family, even his vocation to keep the young English girl in his life. But slowly, insidiously, something else also began. A strange chemistry of place and passion — Paris and love — had set in motion another life and another relationship, an emotion stronger than anything Vicky had ever known before, stronger than life itself.

Forget Me Not is a love story of startling originality and intensity. Dark, erotic, reaching into a psychic past of aching longing, it brings to life artistry and the uncontainable forces between a man and a woman. Here is a novel which explores romantic fulfilment beyond the confines of a single lifetime and reveals an outstanding storyteller at the peak of her powers.

A Selected List of Fiction Available from Mandarin

While every effort is made to keep prices low, it is sometimes necessary to increase prices at short notice. Mandarin Paperbacks reserves the right to show new retail prices on covers which may differ from those previously advertised in the text or elsewhere.

The prices shown below were correct at the time of going to press.

☐ 7493 0003 5	**Mirage**	James Follett	£3.99
☐ 7493 0134 1	**To Kill a Mockingbird**	Harper Lee	£2.99
☐ 7493 0076 0	**The Crystal Contract**	Julian Rathbone	£3.99
☐ 7493 0145 7	**Talking Oscars**	Simon Williams	£3.50
☐ 7493 0118 X	**The Wire**	Nik Gowing	£3.99
☐ 7493 0121 X	**Under Cover of Daylight**	James Hall	£3.50
☐ 7493 0020 5	**Pratt of the Argus**	David Nobbs	£3.99
☐ 7493 0097 3	**Second from Last in the Sack Race**	David Nobbs	£3.50

All these books are available at your bookshop or newsagent, or can be ordered direct from the publisher. Just tick the titles you want and fill in the form below.

Mandarin Paperbacks, Cash Sales Department, PO Box 11, Falmouth, Cornwall TR10 9EN.

Please send cheque or postal order, no currency, for purchase price quoted and allow the following for postage and packing:

UK	80p for the first book, 20p for each additional book ordered to a maximum charge of £2.00.
BFPO	80p for the first book, 20p for each additional book.
Overseas including Eire	£1.50 for the first book, £1.00 for the second and 30p for each additional book thereafter.

NAME (Block letters) ....

ADDRESS ....

....

....